ALPHA CONTACT

P.K. HAWKINS

SEVERED PRESS
HOBART TASMANIA

ALPHA CONTACT

CHAPTER ONE

As Captain James Bernhard exited his jeep on the way to his "special meeting," he looked up to the clear blue sky over McGinnlas Air Force Base in search of the likely reason he was here. Despite it being the middle of the day, the mysterious object currently orbiting the Earth could still be seen like a single star shining at a time when none should be seen. He wasn't the only one looking, he realized. All around him, any of the Air Force personnel that happened to be out in the hot Nevada sun were doing the same thing. The object had been there for a week now, yet apparently, no one had grown so used to its mysterious presence that they could stop staring up at it in awe.

During the first day that the object had appeared, the entire base had been in emergency stand-by. One week on, the order still stood, and everyone was on edge and curious, but a sense of the normal had returned to the people's daily routines. It was amazing to Bernhard how that could happen. One day, out of nowhere, an obviously constructed object that was not of human origin could appear in low Earth orbit, showing the entire human race once and for all that they were not alone in the universe. Seven days later, people were back to complaining about election ads on TV and wondering if the Cubs had it in them to make it to the World Series again.

Of course, that didn't mean that the world hadn't changed. It just meant that people had a remarkable ability to adapt to it.

Bernhard entered the administration building and stopped at the security checkpoint, which was understandably tighter than it had ever been in the past. And security at McGinnlas was always tighter than normal. This place had been the site of many top secret tests over the years, or so it was rumored. In truth, quite a bit of what went on here was above Bernhard's security clearance. But even without most of that knowledge, Bernhard had a pretty good idea of why he had been called in to see Lieutenant General Novak. The only surprising thing was that he hadn't been called in sooner.

It was probably because of petty bureaucracy. That was always the reason things got done slower than they should.

After clearing security, Bernhard was led down several non-descript hallways to an elevator that could only be accessed by handprints. From there, his escorts took him down several floors to a subbasement that probably wasn't supposed to exist, and then through several more boring, unadorned hallways before they brought him into the lieutenant general's office. Like everything else in the building so far, the office was drab and completely lacking in decoration. There was nothing about it that said Novak did business here on a regular basis. This could only be a temporary set-up based on the current state of emergency.

Novak, who had been going over several papers on his desk, stood up at Bernhard's entrance. Bernhard's two security escorts quietly left the room and shut the door, audibly engaging the lock behind them. Bernhard stood at attention and saluted.

"Lieutenant General," Bernhard said.

"At ease, Captain," Novak said. He gestured at a chair in front of his desk. "Please sit. Normally, I would explain to you why I've called you here, but I'm sure by now you already have a pretty good guess."

"Yes, sir," Bernhard said. "I would believe that word has finally officially come down from the president regarding what we're to do regarding the, uh, object."

"Officially, it's being dubbed in all our documents as Object 1156-C, but really, no one is calling it that. The news media has apparently come to the consensus that it's to be called the Visitor. Not terribly creative, I know, but there are a lot worse things it could be called. If we had let people on the internet name it, they'd be calling it Alien McShippenstein or some other such nonsense. But you're correct. An official course of action has finally been decided upon. You'll have to forgive me, though. I know a lot of what I'm about to say is public knowledge already, but I have to make sure this briefing is completely by the book. You understand, I'm sure."

"Absolutely, sir. There's too much riding on all of this. I get that you're going to need to make sure your ass is covered."

"Indeed," Novak said. He slid a copy of a file folder across the desk to Bernhard. It had the obligatory *Top Secret – Eyes Only* stamp, although Bernhard doubted that the intelligence within included much that hadn't already been discussed ad nauseum by late night talk show hosts. That lack of detailed, privileged information was, after all, exactly the reason Bernhard believed he was here.

Bernhard opened the folder and perused the first reports on top of the stack inside.

"The Visitor appeared in low Earth orbit at 0946 hours Greenwich Mean Time, six days ago," Novak said. "Weight and length of the object are difficult to determine, as it appears to include some kind of stealth technology that confounds even basic video devices. Basically, the only way anyone has been able to get a look at it at all has been through telescopes. And even that effort is made more difficult due to the fact that it is maintaining a geosynchronous orbit that always keeps it on the day-side of the planet except for a period of roughly eight minutes after sunset. That it's a made object rather than naturally occurring is not in doubt, given what we've been able to see regarding its shape and proportions. No country or group on Earth has taken credit for its existence, so the assumption is that it is extra-terrestrial in origin."

Bernhard nodded along with all this. This was still within the realm of things that everyone knew. Now was the point where Novak would start giving him more privileged information.

"All major countries throughout the entire world have been involved in closed-door meetings since the beginning of the Visitor's appearance. At this point, it has done nothing to give us the impression that it is hostile, yet all attempts at contacting it have failed. I'm sure you've already seen that, among certain groups, the Visitor's presence has been an agitating force. There was that cult in Ohio four days ago, as well as the growing unrest in Russia and India due to certain charismatic opportunists. What you are probably not so aware of, although maybe you have suspected, is that a number of countries are prepared to go to war over this."

"It did occur to me that such a thing was likely, sir," Bernhard said. "Not that I completely understand the motivations."

"Just between you and me, Bernhard, anyone who talks that political-science mumbo jumbo about motivations is full of bullshit. There are powerful countries, and there are not so powerful countries that want to pretend they are. All of them see this as an unprecedented opportunity to flex their muscles and act mighty."

"Included the U.S., I'm assuming," Bernhard said.

"Even if we didn't want to, we'd have to. Everyone's got their militaries on stand-by, and intelligence seems to think that it's not just because some of these countries are preparing to defend against alien attacks like they say they are. Even little countries that no one thinks of as having any power, they're preparing to use this as an excuse to move on any international rival at all in the name of shoring up their defenses. I could go on and on about this, but the base point isn't going to change: there is an alien ship in orbit just hanging out, and until we know why, the political situation throughout the world will destabilize. It has to be addressed."

And this, Bernhard knew, was the core of why he had been invited here today. "We're finally going up to it, aren't we?"

"Yes, we are, but as you can guess, every country in the world wants their own people up there. If someone gets in that ship and discovers that the aliens, if there even are any, want to be allies, then they want their own country to have exclusive access. If anything on the Visitor is not an ally, then they want their own people to take them down, be the heroes, and have first dibs on any technology they might find. And it's pretty much a guarantee at this point that there will be advanced technology. If the wrong people get their hands on something like, say, some kind of interstellar warp drive device, then they're the ones who become the new super power in the world."

"And that's why it's taken so long for us to consider sending anyone up, isn't it?" Bernhard asked. "Treaties have to be formed. Vows not to use any violent technology against other countries, and promises to share anything that might be otherwise useful."

"That's exactly correct. You should hear some of the garbage coming out of the world politicians' mouths at this point, except most of it is so classified I'd be tried for treason for telling you. Suffice it to say, there's a lot of grown people out there acting like spoiled children. But now there's an agreement. It hasn't even been announced to the public yet, and the White House is trying to keep the specifics of the agreement under wraps until the mission is well underway."

Much of this was included in the first couple pages of the folder, although in much more formal language with lots of buzz-words. After Bernhard flipped through those initial parts of the file, he came to the stuff he really needed to know.

"The US and China are working together to take point on this, it looks like," Bernhard said.

Novak nodded. "With England, India, Australia, and South Africa all taking a large part in the set up and behind the scenes work."

"No Russia?" Bernhard asked.

Novak smirked. "The reason they aren't participating is classified, which is a shame, considering how amusing it is." The smile disappeared from his face just as quickly as it had appeared. "Given the breakdown in relations with Russia over this, the Soyuz vehicles we've been using to send astronauts to the International Space Station for the past two decades won't be feasible for this mission, not to mention that the large amount of manpower and equipment that needs to be sent up wouldn't fit anyway. So, for this mission, we're pulling out one of the old mothballed Space Shuttles."

Bernhard whistled. "Is it even safe to still use those things?"

"No, and it's going to be even less safe considering how rushed this operation is being put together."

Bernhard nodded. He'd had enough Air Force buddies go over to NASA to know that any space mission, no matter how small or insignificant, took an insane amount of planning. And now the eggheads in charge were being expected to set one up in...

"When is this mission happening?" Bernhard asked.

"You're going up tomorrow," Novak said.

Bernhard tried not to act shocked. Not only was that kind of timetable next to impossible to set up safely, but he hadn't fully expected to actually be part of the team that went up to the Visitor. He'd known he would be involved in some way, but he'd expected to be part of training the group that went up or as some other form of ground support.

"Is that going to be a problem, Captain?" Novak asked.

"No, sir. It's just highly unusual, is all."

"Yeah, well, name one part of this whole thing that isn't highly unusual," Novak said. "The entire world was caught with their pants down around their ankles on this one. Once upon a time, the US government had contingency plans set up for possible alien contact, if it ever happened. But such a thing has been neglected over the last couple of presidents, and not because of anything to do with political parties, either. Plain and simple, no one believed this was anywhere in the realm of possibility, and any efforts to plan for it were a waste of time and money. Now we've had to dig deep within our archives to find old plans to deal with first contact with an alien species, then remove all the references to outdated equipment and political boundaries and whatnot."

"So what you're saying, sir, if I may speak freely, is that the plan I currently have in my hand is a cobbled together Frankenstein-monster that will likely blow up in our faces at some point."

"Officially, I have to deny that and say that I have the utmost faith in everyone that drafted the Alpha Contact Contingency. Unofficially, hell yeah. This is going to be a shit-fest of epic proportions."

CHAPTER TWO

Outside Bernhard's quarters in Florida, where he had been transported to immediately following his meeting with Novak, he could hear chaos as orders were shouted, heavy equipment was moved about, and people called out confused questions in both English and Chinese. This was what happened when a hastily thrown together international operation had to be ready to go with only twenty-two hours to go until launch time. Bernhard knew chaos well. He'd trained for it. But the chaos he could deal with was in battle or while flying. A massive sea of human bodies being ordered around by diplomats with no clue about military operations? Not so much.

In his bunk, Bernhard lay back on the sheets, fitted in a pair of ear buds, then cued up some Ozzy Osbourne on his MP3 player. As much as others might make fun of him for it, Ozzy was his go-to when he needed to calm down, concentrate, or just meditate on his life. The early post-Black Sabbath stuff especially, with Randy Rhodes' scorching guitar solos, worked best to set his mind at ease. As the opening chords of "Bark at the Moon" began, Bernhard opened up the folder again and once more poured over its contents. He, for better or worse, was going to be the commanding officer on this mission, and although he sincerely hoped it would be quiet and calm, he needed to be prepared and knowledgeable just case it wasn't.

While he was nominally in charge of the entire group that would be going up to the Visitor, his main command was of the 843rd Special Operations Squadron, or at least those three other members of the squadron that would be accompanying him. He'd worked with those three men – Bart Hodges, Aaron McNeil, and Daniel Zersky – many times before, and he trusted their abilities. It was everyone else on the team for the Alpha Contact Contingency that was unknown to him. And there were a decent number of people; more than he was comfortable bringing.

The American military contingent consisted of the four from Special Operations, as well as three Army Rangers: Mark Sorensen, Daniel Stroebel, and Justin Hatch. While Mark Sorensen was nominally in charge of the rangers, Novak had been clear that Bernhard was the highest in the American chain of command. While the various branches of the military could sometimes butt heads with each other, it had been decided from higher in command that it was most likely that the mission would require a mix of Air Force Spec Ops and Army Rangers, so there was no helping it. Bernhard simply had to hope that everyone would play nice together.

The Chinese contingent consisted of six people, although Bernhard had very little information on them other than their surnames: Teng, Chow, Ngai, Yeow, Taam, and Tshien. He didn't even know which branch of the Chinese military they represented. Apparently, this had been one of the conditions the Chinese had set in exchange for letting the Americans take charge in other areas. Especially with so many countries throughout the world suddenly at each other's throats, China wanted to keep their own capabilities and tactics as secretive as possible. Had they all been able to plan the Alpha Contact Contingency further in advance, the US would probably have more intelligence regarding who these people were and what they could do.

Bernhard rubbed his head. He saw so many ways in which this whole mission was a recipe for disaster, but there was nothing that could be done for it.

And none of that even took into consideration the civilians that would be coming up to the Visitor with them. Bernhard was about to go over their info again when he heard a knock at his door. He turned the music down, pulled out his ear buds, and sat up on the edge of his bed. "Come in."

He recognized the face of the woman who entered right away from the file, although it took him a second to remember her name. Jane Johnson. Right. With a name like that, no wonder he had trouble remembering it. Innocuous name aside, she was going to be an important part of this mission, and Bernhard was suddenly glad for this opportunity to meet the lead science advisor for the American side before they went up.

It also didn't hurt that she was absolutely beautiful.

Not that she likely believed that. She had that mousy way about her that said she wasn't entirely aware of her looks. She had long black hair pulled into a tight ponytail and thick glasses, as well as a white lab coat. Something about that struck Bernhard as funny. He'd thought scientists in white coats was just an outdated stereotype, but apparently, he was wrong.

"Dr. Johnson," Bernhard said as he stood up and offered his hand. She took it, although he felt the way her hand shook nervously. Maybe she was skittish about meeting him, but it seemed much more likely that she was wracked with excitement and fear regarding what they were all about to do. He couldn't blame her.

"Captain Bernhard," Johnson said. "I know that we're supposed to meet at the mission briefing, but I was hoping I could talk to you alone first. If you have a minute?"

"Sure. Did you want to go to the canteen for this?" Not that he actually wanted to go out into that sea of craziness out there just yet, but he was sure the woman would be more comfortable talking in public than she would be here in his room that consisted of little more than a bed and a desk.

She surprised him, though. "Actually, I don't think you want us to be in public for this?" She said it like a question, as though he somehow knew what she was going to ask already and wanted his opinion on it before he even knew she was here. He found it cute, if a little strange.

"Why don't you sit down?" Bernhard asked, motioning at the desk chair. She took a seat, her foot immediately tapping in a rapid staccato movement against the floor. Either she was really nervous being here, or else it was just some kind of personal tick. Bernhard sat at the edge of his bed. "How can I help you?"

"I... I wanted to talk to you about the nuclear device," Johnson said. She wouldn't look him in the eye, which made it easier for him to hide his surprise.

"I'm sorry. I don't know what you're talking about," Bernhard said.

"I like movies."

Bernhard paused, unsure how he was supposed to respond to that. He knew that scientists had a reputation, not always earned, of being odd, but this was just plain baffling. "Uh, okay. I'm not sure what..."

"I like all kinds of movies," she said. Finally, she looked at him with a bizarre intensity. "I like action movies. Sci-fi movies. Superhero movies. Things like that."

"I'm still not..."

"In movies, something big or strange happens," Johnson said. "Like some kind of creature shows up, or something magical happens, and no one knows what to do about it. People get scared. The military gets called in."

Bernhard thought he was beginning to understand the point this strange woman was trying to make. "You're not happy that the first thing we're doing when a potential alien ship appears in orbit is to send a military strike team, are you?"

"I understand why that's necessary," Johnson said. "I don't like it, but I understand. I would love to think that this is first contact and there are some extra-terrestrials aboard the Visitor that is going to bring us a new era of peace on Earth. But if that's wrong, that's what you guys are there for. I get that."

"But there's still something you're uncomfortable about, isn't there?" Bernhard prompted.

Johnson nodded. "In the movies, there's always some kind of backup. A way to destroy everything if something goes wrong. The military will attack the creature or the ship with something. If they're afraid of it enough, the thing they attack with is some kind of nuclear weapon. There's always a nuclear weapon in these situations. And it's always a terrible mistake. It makes the creature stronger, or the aliens turn it around on the good guys."

"Okay. I see where you're coming from, Dr. Johnson. But this isn't the movies. We're not taking some kind of nuclear bomb up to the Visitor."

"Of course that's what you would say," Johnson said. "And I don't blame you for lying to me. But I know it's part of the plan. It always is."

"Dr. Johnson, maybe this isn't the kind of thing you should be talking with me about," Bernhard said. "If you're that convinced there's some secret agenda to destroy the Visitor, you should talk about this with the people who planned this mission."

"If I did that, I would probably get kicked off the mission. They would think I'm being too paranoid."

"But you don't expect me to believe that?"

"No, because you know the truth. We're going to be sent up there with some kind of bomb, probably nuclear, and you're going to be expected to use it if anything doesn't go according to plan. I'm asking you not to."

"If you're concerned about your safety…"

"I'm not. Sure, I don't want to die in a nuclear explosion, but that's not why I'm asking you not to do it. Whatever the Visitor is, whatever we find up there, it's the greatest scientific find in all human history. You can't destroy it."

"Okay, look. There's no nuclear bomb going up with us. And trust me, if there were, I would know. But just let me play devil's advocate here. What if we get up there and we don't just find superior technology, but we find a clear and present threat to humanity. You honestly think the best course of action would be to not destroy it?"

"Why would the only options be destroying it or not destroying it? I guess all I'm asking you is to not just assume that the situation is going to be black and white. Even if we find something bad, imagine all the good that might come out of it."

"You know, when a beautiful woman walks into my bedroom, this is hardly the kind of conversation I expect to have."

Dr. Johnson blinked several times. "I don't understand what you mean."

No, Bernhard realized. She didn't. She didn't understand the awkwardness here, nor did she seem to realize that Bernhard found her at all attractive. All in all, that was probably for the best. No one on this mission could afford to think of anything other than the task at hand.

"Well, let me just say it one more time. There is no bomb. That is not part of the plan. But even if there were, I would take your advice into consideration."

"That's all I ask," she said. Without further ado, she stood up and walked out the door, not even bothering to say good-bye.

Bernhard closed his door, locked it, and then went back to his bed and the file. That had been a thoroughly perplexing conversation for many reasons, but the biggest reason of all was that she was one hundred percent right. They *were* being sent up to the Visitor with a nuclear bomb. And if anything at all went wrong, he'd been ordered to detonate it. It was supposed to be a secret known only to him. Not even anyone in the Chinese contingent was to know about it.

And yet this woman had simply walked in and deduced the bomb's existence purely because she watched too many movies. Bernhard was going to need to keep a close eye on her. He was also going to have to do his damnedest not to like her.

CHAPTER THREE

The next twenty-four hours were a whirlwind of preparation for everyone. There were briefings to give to the Alpha Contact team, and due to secrecy reasons, each of the four branches of the team – American military, American science, Chinese military, and Chinese science – were given slightly different information. No one was exactly given wrong information, but Bernhard had been given very careful instructions regarding which people were allowed to know what. This was followed immediately by extensive medical and psychological testing for everyone. All of that, under normal circumstances, would have been done much earlier, and anyone who failed even the smallest test would have been expected to leave the mission. With time of the essence and the political situation what it was, though, a lot of medical leeway was given. One of the scientists on the Chinese side apparently had mild asthma, but the hastily signed agreements between nations had been adamant that he was allowed as part of the mission. One of the American scientists was diabetic, while Johnson's terrible eyesight should have also disqualified her for any space mission.

Bernhard tried to take it all in stride, even though his worry about the state of things got worse by the minute.

Everyone went through as much space mission training as could possibly be fit into such a short period of time. Again, on the military side, most of the team members did well here. The scientists, unused to that level of physical stress, vomited early and often. Bernhard had a horrible vision of everyone floating in zero-g amid of cloud of partially digested food.

Finally, the time came where they were all to be loaded on the shuttle. As they approached the enormous craft with its giant fuel tank and booster rockets, Bernhard felt a little queasy himself. This equipment had been in storage for far too long, and the rigorous safety checks that normally would have been a part of such a mission had likely been reduced to only the bare essentials. Bernhard had flown in many aircraft before, including several that the United States would publicly deny even existed, but never had he felt this level of nerves as he walked up to the facility to be outfitted with his suit.

"You are nervous," someone said next to him in a heavy Chinese accent. Bernhard turned to see Teng, commander on the Chinese military side. They'd met briefly yesterday, but there hadn't been time to exchange anything more than polite hellos.

"I don't know that I'd say I'm nervous."

"I can tell that you are, but that is fine. I am too." Teng gestured at the shuttle. "Just look at that thing. It is older than my mother."

Bernhard couldn't help but smile. "Your people didn't have anything more modern or suitable?"

Teng smiled back. "That is classified."

For this particular mission, the un-retired space shuttle had been renamed the *Ambassador*. As with so much else regarding the mission, it was a patched-together monstrosity on the inside, as the engineers in charge of getting them all into space and back without dying had needed to basically gut it to fit all their gear and personnel. While all the scientists wore traditional astronaut jumpsuits, the military people were all already dressed for combat. If they got up to the Visitor and, immediately upon docking with it, they were rushed by alien soldiers, it wouldn't do for them to have to try to equip themselves in zero-g. Once everyone else was on the *Ambassador* and strapped into their seats, Bernhard, Teng, and Zersky came on last. Zersky, having had previous experience with piloting certain experimental aircraft, would be their pilot, responsible for getting them to the Visitor, as well as hopefully docking them safely and later getting them back to Earth. Bernhard and Teng, as the leaders of the two contingents, were expected to come on last purely for looks. Bernhard noticed as they came on and climbed into their sideways seats that cameras had been set up throughout the shuttle in addition to the body cameras that every single person was expected to keep turned on at all times. Bernhard knew that mostly this was for monitoring purposes, since Novak would be on the ground, hopefully able to communicate with them if he saw anything he didn't like, but a part of him was pretty sure that, with the mess that this mission had already proved to be before they'd even taken off, something from those cameras would end up on the news networks at some point. Hell, even with the top of the line encryptions the military would be using for the video signals, someone had probably already hacked it and was streaming the entire thing throughout the world.

"Are you okay?" Johnson asked Bernhard as he took his seat.

"I'm fine."

"You're lying again."

He ignored the "again" part. "Maybe my thoughts are just top secret."

"Don't you ever think that all the secrecy we're trying to put on this mission is only going to make things worse?" she asked.

"No, I don't. There are always going to be some things that some people shouldn't know."

"Just like that one thing we talked about?"

One of the other American scientists, Houston, turned to look at them. "What one thing?" he asked.

"There is no one thing," Bernhard said, doing his best to hide his exasperation. "And if there was a one thing, it wouldn't be your one thing to know, Houston. Remember that." He looked at Johnson and spoke to her as quietly as he could, which was made more difficult by the growing roar of the preparations of the ship around them. "Let it all go, Johnson. That's an order."

"All the secrecy won't do anything to help," Johnson said. "Not in here with the team, and not out there in the world. You may be used to everything and its mother being classified, but any real chance of keeping secrets about any of this vanished the moment the Visitor appeared in orbit. It would be better for everyone to be in the know from the beginning."

"We're not having this conversation anymore, Johnson. Now finish your prep. Launch is in less than fifteen minutes."

"Oh my God. I can't believe we're doing this," Houston said. "We're actually going to space. To visit an alien space ship. In space!"

The third and last American scientist, a woman by the name of Patricia Dufresne, spoke up. "Houston, are we going to have a problem here?"

"Ha ha, Trish," Houston said. "That's hilarious. Really. I've never heard that joke in my entire life."

"Was that sarcasm?"

"Yes, Trish. It was sarcasm."

"Oh come on. Just because you've heard that joke before doesn't mean it's not funnier under the current situation."

"Oh dear Lord," Sorensen muttered. He was sitting directly next to Bernhard, and he leaned closer so that only Bernhard could hear him. "Are we going to have to listen to these people all the way into orbit?"

Bernhard had to admit that he wasn't particularly fond of that possibility, either. "Alright, everyone, knock it off."

"Or what?" Dufresne asked. "You're going to turn this shuttle around and take us right home?"

Bernhard shot an embarrassed look in Teng's direction. All of Teng's people, scientists included, had loaded up onto the *Ambassador* in complete silence and with perfect efficiency. Teng saw the look and smiled, but still said nothing.

Babysitting, Bernhard decided. This mission was going to be mostly babysitting of the American scientists. It was a distinct relief when everything was ready and the countdown finally began. At lift off, the scientists finally shut up as the g-forces made it more or less impossible for them to do more than grimace for the entire time it took them to leave Earth's gravitational pull. Only then did Bernhard allow himself to think again about the likelihood that this old museum-piece of a spacecraft would likely disintegrate underneath them before they reached the outer atmosphere. At this point, such a thing would have almost been a relief. Their deaths would be quick, and it meant that Bernhard wouldn't have to deal with unruly and undisciplined people anymore.

That was also the moment Bernhard realized he'd never actually called his daughter and listened to her voice one more time, just in case. Not that he would have been allowed to tell her or her mother where he was going. The media wasn't going to be told they'd gone up until after the *Ambassador* was floating in the void around the planet. But it bothered him that he hadn't even considered talking to her. Was he really getting that distant? More importantly, did she even care anymore?

They could all feel the moment the *Ambassador* was free of its tank and booster rockets, then soon after, the disorientation hit them all as their world lost gravity. This, apparently, was the cue to Houston, Dufresne, and Johnson to talk again. While Houston and Dufresne joked about whether or not the captain was going to turn off the "fasten seatbelts" sign, Johnson looked over at Bernhard and spoke quietly to him.

"Penny for your thoughts, Captain Bernhard?"

"No."

"How about a twenty?"

At that, Bernhard couldn't help but smile, no matter how hard he tried not to. "That's a hell of an inflation rate."

"If you take me up on it, you'll have to wait to collect until we get back to Earth. I think I forgot my purse in my car."

He laughed. Both Houston and Dufresne stopped talking for a moment at the unexpected noise. When Bernhard shot them a dirty look, they went back to ignoring him and instead snarking at each other.

"I think you scared them for a second there, Captain."

"Johnson, it's not like I've never laughed before."

"Could have fooled me. Now, you want to share why you were looking so pensive there for a while?"

"No."

Johnson looked over at Hodges and McNeil. "You two have worked with him before, right? What's it take to get him to share?"

"Share? I'm not sure that Bernhard knows what that word means," McNeil said.

"Sure he does," Hodges said. "He's shared something personal with me before. It was, um, hmm, now just hold on. I know there must have been something."

Bernhard had no problem with their lighthearted-ribbing, but the last thing he wanted was for Johnson to hear that and think she could join in. She had already managed to get beneath his skin more than he was comfortable with. "Can it, you two. That's a direct order."

"Okay everyone," Zersky announced back to them. "We're coming up on the approach with the Visitor in just under twenty minutes. Teng, Bernhard, Johnson, and Xiang, you guys better get to the cockpit. We're going to need to start making decisions on what to do and how to approach it as soon as it's in visual range."

The four of them unbelted from their seats. Bernhard had done zero-g training before on the Air Force jet often affectionately known as the Vomit Comet, so he was the one who was most at ease once he was floating free in the air. Teng, apparently, had received some similar training at some point, as he wasn't that bad either. Xiang, head of the Chinese science team, moved awkwardly at first but soon seemed to know what he was doing. It was only Johnson who hopelessly flailed for a bit as she had to learn that even the slightest bump against anything could send her moving in exactly the opposite direction she wanted to go. When she temporarily got stuck near the back of the cabin, Bernhard finally took pity on her and followed her back, then took a minute to show her how to use everything in her environment as either a hand grip or something which she could push off of with her feet.

"Thanks," Johnson said once they were both in the cockpit with the others. "It never looks that hard on TV."

Bernhard watched the way her hair floated in a halo behind her head, and the way her glasses, now that she had put them back on after takeoff, constantly threatened to float away from her face. It was cute, in a way that…

"Hello?" Johnson asked. "Bernhard? Are you still with me?"

"Um, yes. Sure. You're welcome."

Doing his best to ignore any more inappropriate thoughts, Bernhard turned his attention to the cockpit window and the thing they were just now starting to see.

Xiang said something in Mandarin Chinese. Bernhard spoke some Mandarin, but he wouldn't have needed a translator to understand the distinct notes of awe and wonder in Xiang's voice. Bernhard felt the exact same thing, although he wasn't about to allow himself to show any such emotion. It had been evident from everything else that had happened in the last week that the Visitor was obviously alien in origin, but only now, as he was finally seeing it unaided and growing closer, did the momentousness of this situation start to overwhelm him.

Humans weren't alone in the universe. There was indeed something else out there. And for one reason or another, that something had chosen now to show up on their doorstep.

Then another thought occurred to him, something that had been in the back of his mind before now, but which he hadn't allowed himself to really recognize until now. He might be the first one to set foot on the Visitor, assuming they found a way to access it. Even if he wasn't the first, he would be among the first small group. Was this was Neil Armstrong had felt like when he was the first to step on the moon? Would Bernhard's name go down in history as one of the great explorers?

Bernhard was surprised when he felt sadness at the understanding that it likely would not. So much of this mission was supposed to be shrouded in secrecy, after all. If everything went according to the way the Air Force intended, his participation here would likely stay hidden for a long time. And again, to his surprise, he felt a little resentment at that. Not so much that he would be a silent player in all this. He could accept that part. He'd been a quiet part of many tasks and missions as part of Spec Ops and it had never bothered him before. Secrecy was part of the job, and if his country wanted him to sacrifice some of the glory, he would gladly do it.

But Bernhard wondered about his daughter. Was she down there on Earth somewhere, staring up at the Visitor? Would she ever know that her father had been a part of this? Or would she always just believe that he had once again neglected to call her, that she meant nothing to him, that other things in his life came before his actual flesh and blood?

Bernhard looked over to see Johnson staring at him again. He tried to ignore her.

"So what have we got?" Bernhard asked, making sure that his personal body camera was recording not just what he saw but everything he said.

"All digital attempts to view or record the Visitor are still being confounded," Zersky said. "We're going to all have to make sure we describe what we see, in case it doesn't get picked up on the recordings."

"It looks very flat," Teng said. "Like it is just a wall hanging in space."

"If it's a ship," Johnson said, "then whoever designed it has a very different concept of what works and what doesn't than what we do. Aerodynamically, it doesn't look like it could move."

"Look at the far end, though," Xiang said in English this time. "That might be some kind of thrusters. A method of propulsion."

"All of that's well and good," Bernhard said. "But what we really need to find is a way in. There has to be some kind of airlock. That's our first priority."

"Details are a bit fuzzy from here," Zersky said. "We'll have to get closer to actually search it."

"Hey!" Dufresne called from the back. "When do we get a chance to see? We came all this way, so we have a right to science, too!"

Bernhard looked to Johnson. "Those two are going to be lucky if I don't throttle them before any of us get back to Earth."

Johnson patiently patted him on the shoulder. "Go easy on them. Houston is a brilliant engineer and Dufresne is one of the foremost botanists on the planet."

"Yeah, about that," Zersky asked. "Why the hell did we bring a botanist, anyway?"

"Because we don't even have the slightest clue where we're going to need to begin with this thing," Johnson said. "The Visitor might be some kind of ark for alien plant life. Or it might be a very high-tech message in a bottle, some way for the aliens to test out if there's anything out in the void."

"Or it could be a warship," Bernhard added.

"Or an intergalactic advertisement for orange juice!" Dufresne called back. "You guys do know I can totally hear you talking about me, right?"

Bernhard stopped talking. This was going to be a long first contact.

CHAPTER FOUR

Even up close, the Visitor continued to resist any and all attempts to record it. Even their individual body cameras, when pointed in the direction of the mysterious alien object through the window, would start to whine with interference.

"That might cause a problem when we get inside the Visitor," Bernhard said.

"If we can get inside at all," Teng said.

"Look over there," Xiang said, pointing at a point about halfway up this side of the Visitor. "There is a depression in the side. It might be a door."

"Zersky, get us closer to it and see if we can get a better look," Bernhard said. He turned around and called back to the others. "Houston, get up here. This might be where we need some engineering skills." Teng, likewise, had his own mechanical engineering expert, a woman named Li, come up and join them. It was starting to get rather crowded in the cockpit, but then there was nothing to help it. These kinds of problems were exactly why the scientists were here, after all, so Bernhard needed as many of the big brains working together on this.

"Is the Visitor giving off any kind of signal?" Li asked as they got closer to what they hoped was the main entrance.

"Nothing that our instruments are reading," Bernhard said. "Why? What are you thinking?"

"There might be some kind of call and response," Houston chimed in. "That's what you're alluding to, right?"

"Correct," Li said. "I thought it might be waiting for some kind of code in order to open."

"Maybe there is a signal, but just not using any wavelength or technology we recognize," Johnson said.

"Zersky, see if this thing is emitting something else other than radio waves," Bernhard said. "Check radiation, maybe."

"Negative on radiation," Zersky said.

Xiang seemed to be interested at that. "You mean no radiation being intentionally sent out, right?"

"No, I'm mean I'm not picking up any radiation at all," Zersky said. "That's what we want, isn't it? I know I sure don't want to get on that thing and suddenly get enough of a dose to start growing a third testicle."

"Gross!" Johnson said. Li, on the other hand, gave Zersky an appreciative look like she might want to see that.

"It would not make any sense for there to be no radiation," Xiang said. "Wherever this thing came from, it has traveled a great distance, likely through space. Even if it managed to skip through all that space through something like a wormhole, it should still show slightly higher than normal radiation purely for being out here for as long as it has."

"Let me run another test and see," Zersky said. "Uh, no. Nothing. You're right. I'm not even picking up the slightest background radiation from it."

"Almost like it's absorbing the radiation," Johnson said.

"All of this is very fascinating, I'm sure, but does anyone have any ideas on if this information will help us actually get in?"

"Wait, look!" Teng said, pointing out the window. As they got closer to the depression in the side of the Visitor, they got a better sense of scale. The huge size of the mysterious alien object had made it difficult for them to tell from far away, but the closer they got, the more they realized this wasn't merely some small door or airlock. This was big, like the open door of a hangar. Bernhard's mind immediately went back to McGinnlas Air Base, where a huge hangar inevitably meant fighter jets. He couldn't think of any reason why a ship on some kind of mission of peace would need a hangar door that size.

He thought back to the nuclear device, quietly hiding away in their cargo along with the rest of their gear, where it was inside a lead-lined box. Thinking of an invading army of alien fighters, he made sure to mentally go over the codes for the bomb one more time. Just in case.

But that wasn't even what had caught Teng's attention. Again, because of the scale, Bernhard hadn't seen at first. It had simply looked like there was a dark line painted at the bottom of the door. It wasn't until he saw the line thickening that he realized it was opening.

"Stop the *Ambassador*," Bernhard said. "Don't get any closer."

"What, are you crazy?" Houston asked. "That's exactly what we've –"

"Shut up," Bernhard said. "As much as you people want to act like this is some kind of amazing vacation, all of this is still a military operation, and I am in command." He looked back at Zersky. "Maintain a safe distance. Wait until the door is open all the way, then do further scans and tests. For all we know, that could be some kind of Death Star super laser, and if we try to fly in, it might fry us all."

"Affirmative, Captain," Zersky said.

"You don't really think that's what it is, do you?" Johnson asked.

"No. But it doesn't matter what I think it is. We are going to do everything proper and by the book up until we know for sure. And Johnson, just because I like you doesn't mean you can question my decisions, do you understand?"

"You like me?"

"No. Go back to your seat." He nodded at Teng. "What you want your people to do is up to you, but as mission leader, I highly suggest getting anyone you think is non-essential for this part strapped back in and prepared for the possibility of something coming out of that door."

Teng nodded. "Xiang, go on back. Li, you stay."

Fifteen minutes later, Bernhard was forced to admit that his caution was unwarranted. None of their instruments picked up anything out of the ordinary, except for the curious continued lack of background radiation. Bernhard kept note of that, then instructed Zersky to approach the hangar door. Still, he didn't have them go in.

"Whatever kind of stealth or jamming technology this thing has," Zersky said, "it seems to be worse inside. From the outside, it was giving us scrambled visuals. But all cameras are pointed to look in and picking up nothing at all. Just blackness."

And everyone in the cockpit could see very well that the hangar was, in fact, well lit. There were lights running along the walls, illuminating what appeared to be hundreds of boxes hanging from the ceiling. The floor, on the other hand, looked empty.

No, Bernhard realized. That wasn't the floor at all. That was the ceiling. Drifting here in space, it was easy to get disoriented compared to other objects. To them, the Visitor almost appeared to be upside down, but really it was the other way. Those boxes hanging from ceiling were actually on the floor, which implied...

"There's gravity inside there," Bernhard said.

Houston pointed outside the hangar at the Visitor itself. "The Visitor isn't rotating or anything like that."

Bernhard looked at him. "And why do you seem to think that's significant?"

Li spoke up. "When we put something into space, if we want to simulate gravity in a weightless environment, we would have the object rotating. The spin would seem to act in the same way as gravity to anyone and anything inside it."

Houston nodded. "But if the Visitor isn't doing that, then that means the gravity we're seeing inside this hangar is generated in some other way. We're looking at true artificial gravity. That right there, all by itself, is a new technology that could completely change the course of the human race."

"How so?" Bernhard asked.

"To start with, it could be used to minimize the effects of atrophy on anyone we send into space," Houston said. "If we all sat in this shuttle for long enough, our muscles would begin to suffer from not having to deal with gravity all the time. If we had this tech, it could make it more feasible for humans to be part of long-distance space travel, even without any kind of long-distance traveling device. It would theoretically be able to give us –"

"Okay, okay, I get it," Bernhard said. He didn't need to know all the theoretical ways this technology could change the world. All he needed to know was that it was valuable, and every major nation and corporation throughout the world would want to get their hands on it. "Zersky, I guess that means that if we're going to try to land in there, we'll need to flip the *Ambassador* to orient with it."

"Is that the official order then, Captain?"

"It is."

"Okay. Then just to let you know, these old space shuttles weren't built for that kind of landing. It's designed for a long stop, just like a jet. There's no vertical take-off or landing ability."

Bernhard understood what that meant. Shuttles were supposed to dock with objects in space, not land on them. Not only would it be difficult and strange to set the *Ambassador* down inside, but it would be even harder for them to leave again without any kind of runway.

Escape, if they needed to do it, would be tough.

"Your concern is understood and noted," Bernhard said. "Do what you need to do to land us in there. Everyone, back to your seats. You don't want to be floating in the air when we cross over into that hangar and gravity returns."

Bernhard went back with the others and took his seat, but not before he once again checked his weapons and equipment. No one else had noticed, or at least mentioned, it yet, but considering that the door had opened for them with no outside input, the implication was that something else had done it for them. Despite the total lack of communication they'd had so far, there was someone or something in there that was aware of their presence. The opening of the door for them could be a friendly overture, or it could be the setup for an ambush. Let the scientists hope for the former. He and his men would prepare for the latter.

CHAPTER FIVE

Dr. Johnson did this thing when she was nervous where she bit her lip. Bernhard found it cute, which annoyed him.

"I still think this is a bad idea," Johnson said.

"And I still agree with you," Bernhard replied. "Why are we still going over this?"

"Because you're the commander of this mission. You can make an order and have it done differently."

It was exactly the same conversation they'd been having for the last fifteen minutes, just with different words each time. They were all preparing to exit the *Ambassador*, and Johnson had been voicing her disapproval of this the whole time, although at least now she had the decency and courtesy to stop questioning him in front of the others. She'd pulled him aside into the now-empty cockpit for this. Bernhard found it funny that she, with all her talk back on Earth about needing to explore the possibilities of the Visitor before passing judgment on it, was the one saying they shouldn't go out and explore it now.

Granted, she had a lot of very good points. They had done a test of the air inside the Visitor soon after they'd touched down in the hangar, and it had come back as perfectly breathable for humans, with no trace of hazardous gasses or chemicals in the air. Again, that was a bit weird, in that there were none at all even when there should have been at least something in minute traces. But her main argument, and a very good one, was that just because they had searched for hazards that they knew about didn't mean there wasn't something that could hurt them that no one had ever considered before. Most specifically, there was no way to test for alien viruses or bacteria.

Those points, however, were also moot. Plain and simple, they didn't have enough space suits. In any other mission, this would have been a grievous oversight that would get someone fired. In this instance, they had just been some of the many things that they both hadn't been able to get enough of in such a short period of time and also hadn't had the room for. The shuttle had already been dangerously overweight with the things they had no choice but to bring, and decisions had needed to be made quickly. Enough space suits had been packed that someone would have been able to do an extra-vehicular inspection of the Visitor if they hadn't been able to get in. Now that they had made it inside, though, the only way they could use the space suits to guard against hazards was if only a few people wore them while everyone else walked around without, and that was just ridiculous.

Johnson, knowing this was an argument she would never win, eventually went out of the *Ambassador* with everyone else. Bernhard stayed behind long enough to check in on the nuke. It was a small device, relatively low yield, but enough to, if not completely destroy, then at least permanently cripple the Visitor if it came down to that. Bernhard armed the device, then set up the remote detonator he'd been given and hid it on his person. He would be able to activate it from a distance, probably from anywhere within the mysterious alien structure, but it would take a code that only he knew to first turn on the detonator, then another to activate it. While that made it difficult to set off in an emergency, he would rather that be the case than have it possible for him to accidentally bump the detonator in his pocket and blow them all to little radioactive bits.

He walked down the *Ambassador*'s stairs to find that his men, both Army Rangers and Air Force Spec Ops, had done their job and set up a perimeter that they could defend in the event of a sudden attack. Teng's forces had done the same, although Bernhard did notice that the Chinese and the Americans seemed to be keeping their distance from each other. He would have to speak to Teng about that. There might be the occasional tensions between their countries on Earth, but up here everyone needed to remember that they weren't from the US or from China. They were from Earth, all from the same species, and they had to act like it.

From their current vantage point, Bernhard now had a much better idea of the size for the hundreds of boxes in the hangar than he had on their approach. Scale had been difficult to determine then, but now he could see that each box was slightly smaller than the *Ambassador*. They were gray and completely featureless, each of them about fifteen feet high and thirty to forty feet on a side. Zersky had landed the shuttle as far as he could from them, but it was obvious to Bernhard that these had to be the first things they investigated.

"Stroebel, Sorensen, and Hatch. You're with me. Zersky, Hodges, McNeil, stay back for the time being and keep guard on the civilians. Teng, stay back and keep command here, but give me two of your fighters that have a good command of English."

Dufresne immediately started to complain that the scientists should go first when investigating anything regarding technology, but Bernhard had already taken to tuning out every single word she said. Teng, in the meantime, ordered Ngai and Yeow to join up with Bernhard. The two of them fell in easily with the Army Rangers, adapting to their formation and complimenting it with their own, although again they kept their distance. Bernhard took the lead and, with his rifle firmly in hand, they went out and came up to the first of the strange boxes.

At first, the box seemed just as featureless up close as it had from a distance. Up close, though, he saw an incredibly complex configuration of fine lines etched into the outside with geometric precision. It looked similar to the patterns one would see on a circuit board. With the others covering him, Bernhard touched the side of the box, first with the butt of his rifle then the tip, testing it for any kind of trap. The surface remained completely inactive for the moment. Bernhard motioned for them all to go around the side, checking to see that each wall of the box was equally uninteresting.

As it turned out, they were not.

On the side opposite of where they had initially approached, they found a door. Or at least, Bernhard assumed it was a door. The perfectly square depression in the wall looked exactly like a much smaller version of the hangar door. Initially, Bernhard was hesitant to approach it before he remembered the way the hangar door itself had acted. It had remained inert up until the moment the *Ambassador* was almost upon it. Testing a theory, he had Sorensen move slightly closer to the door. Sure enough, as soon as the soldier was within a few feet of it, the door slowly slid up into the side of the box, leaving them an opening. Bernhard silently gestured to signify the position he wanted them all to take inside, then led them all in.

Bernhard was pretty sure, even without the opinion of any of the scientists, that what he saw inside confirmed all of the worst fears of the people that had sent them up here.

As everyone else took up their positions in the event that something popped out at them, Bernhard took a few tentative steps toward the center of the box and the machine it housed.

"Is this what I think it is?" Stroebel asked from his position on the right side of the door.

"That depends," Bernhard said. "Do you think this is some kind of alien fighter ship?"

"That would have been my first guess, Captain, yeah," Stroebel said.

"Then I'd say you're probably right."

While there was no noticeable way for the ship to get out of the box it was stored in, there was no denying at least that they were staring at something that had been designed for fighting and war. The entire thing had a roughly triangular design, and on the underside of the ship there was some kind of bulbous cockpit, held up off the ground by three legs. The top of the ship bristled with various geometric antennas and protrusions, many of which seemed to be pointed in such a way to imply they were weapons. The entire top of the ship, with its strange array, looked like it had been designed by some child who'd thought the only way to make the thing more awesome was to stick more crap on it.

While it didn't look at all like anything an adult human might design for the purpose of war, its intent was obvious to all.

The silent awe with which they all stared at it was interrupted by Sorensen, who jerked and aimed his weapon at Stroebel. "Holy shit, what was that?" Sorensen asked.

Everyone tensed. "What was what?" Bernhard asked.

"Stroebel, you heard that, right? That high-pitched sound right now?"

"Uh, no," Stroebel said. "I didn't."

"I swear I heard it," Sorensen said, although he didn't sound too sure. "It was like a whine. It was right next to my head. Kind of like a mosquito buzzing my ear, but bigger."

"You've got to be hearing things," Stroebel said.

"Maybe it was something with your comm equipment," Bernhard said. "Double check to make sure it's not malfunctioning."

Sorensen tried the radio attached to his uniform, only to find that it wasn't working. Not that it was picking up interference, but that it had stopped working altogether. "Shit," Sorensen said. "You've got to be kidding me. These things aren't supposed to run out of batteries like that, are they?"

Bernhard checked his own, afraid of what he would find. "The same is happening with mine. And it looks like my body camera shut itself off, too."

Every single other person in the room checked their own equipment and found the exact same thing. "It's not a battery problem," Bernhard said. "Everyone out of this room. Back to the others. We'll see if the problem is only with the people that entered this box, or if it's affecting everyone else as well."

They filed out and made their way back to the others. Teng stood ready, his own radio already in his hand.

"Bernhard, there is something wrong," Teng said.

"We noticed the same thing," Bernhard said. "Everything was working fine before we entered the Visitor. There must be something in here that's either draining the power to our electronic equipment, or else the ship is giving off some kind of jamming signal."

"What about what was in the box?" Johnson asked. "Did you find anything?"

"I hate to break this to you, Dr. Johnson, but I do believe that whoever sent the Visitor to us isn't entirely friendly," Bernhard said. "The thing in that box was clearly some kind of personal fighter craft."

"You can't know that for sure," Dufresne said.

"The huge number of weapons sticking out if say otherwise, Dufresne," Bernhard said. "Why don't you do us all a favor and stick to your plants?"

Johnson cleared her throat, clearly disapproving of the tone he took with one of her people, and Bernhard found that he was actually sorry for the outburst. Not because Dufresne didn't deserve to hear it, as she definitely did. Instead, Bernhard didn't like the idea that Johnson might think less of him. Ugh. These kind of feelings were definitely not the sort of thing he needed right now.

"Can we at least see it? This alien fighter craft?" Li asked. "We might be able to tell something about it that none of you could."

"I wouldn't be opposed to that," Bernhard said, "but before that, I want to get a better idea of the layout around here. You know, make sure the owners of these fighters aren't still around somewhere. And until we know that for certain, there will be no further splitting up. With the radios down, we have no way of reaching other groups in the event of an emergency."

"Come on, can't we at least look at it?" Houston asked.

"I am surrounded by children," Bernhard muttered. "No, okay? Either you do as I tell you, or you go back to the ship. Jesus, I can't believe I just said that."

Johnson said something quietly to Houston, but Bernhard was too busy working out a plan with the actual military people to care about what she said to soothe his bruised feelings. Once he felt confident that the various rangers and airmen would adequately be able to protect the civilians, he ordered them out, moving them along the outer walls, hoping they would soon find some door that led to better answers.

CHAPTER SIX

The deeper interior of the Visitor mimicked the same geometric blockiness they saw in the hangar. Whoever had designed this thing, they were big on smooth lines, flat planes, and a complete lack of ornamentation. All the halls were well lit, and the only colors present anywhere were white and gray. The whole thing gave Bernhard the chills, not that he would admit it to anyone.

Johnson, however, wasn't so quiet. "This whole place is pretty spooky. Everything feels dead."

One of the Chinese scientists said something in Mandarin, which Teng translated for the others. "He says there is no dust. If the Visitor was abandoned, there would probably be dust of some kind coating everything."

"Something keeps it clean," Bernhard said. "Or someone."

Dufresne and Houston, thankfully, were just as freaked out by the eerie quiet as everyone else, and therefore kept their mouths shut. One of the Chinese scientists insisted they stop for several minutes in what appeared to be a completely featureless hallway so he could run tests using some equipment Bernhard didn't recognize. When he appeared to be done, Bernhard asked Teng, "Well?"

"He says there is nothing," Teng said. "Still no background radiation. No electromagnetic signals implying power sources, not even near the lights. Obviously, they are being powered by something, but the technology is completely beyond our power or knowledge to detect."

Bernhard nodded. More technology for the people of the world to fight over. While he understood Johnson's point of view about how important these technological leaps could be to humanity, he personally took a much more cynical view. Whichever person, nation, or corporation got their hands on anything they found in the Visitor, they weren't just going to share it. They would use it to hold an advantage over others. Countries would find ways to weaponize it. Of course, his own country would likely be the first in line to do so, but that didn't bother him so much. It was other countries, like if some third-world-dictator someone got control of this alien power technology and kept it for himself, using it to keep his people from rising up against him. Personally, he thought it might be better to destroy it all on general principle. If no one could use it, then no one could misuse it either.

For a second, he wondered what his daughter would think of her father having that sort of cynicism. Of course, at her age, she probably didn't even know what that word meant yet. Hopefully, her mother would keep her innocent of such things for as long as possible.

"There's a depression in the wall up ahead," Li said. "Probably another door."

"Everyone knows the drill by now, I take it?" Bernhard said. "Rangers in the lead. AF Spec Ops protecting the scientists at the rear. Teng, divide your people among the two groups as you see fit."

Bernhard kept just behind the rangers as they approached the door. Like every other door they'd run into so far, it opened by itself once they were close. The rangers flanked the door, then went in with the assumption that something hostile could be waiting on the other side. When Bernhard followed them in with his own weapon at the ready, he found that was exactly the case, just not in any way he had expected.

"Hodges, McNeil, and Zersky, stay outside with the scientists for a minute," Bernhard called out. "Teng, you should get in here with your people. We've got some military decisions to make."

"What? What is it?" Dufresne called from outside. "We have a right to see, too!"

Bernhard ignored her, instead paying attention to Teng's reaction as he entered the room and saw what was inside. Teng gave a low whistle. "This proves it to me," he said. "The Visitor is here with hostile intent."

Bernhard nodded. The room was nothing but a long, wide hallway that went down for maybe five or six hundred yards. On each side, in endless rows, were tubes of some transparent material full of some glowing, light-blue fluid. And suspended within the fluid of each tube was what appeared to be an alien soldier. He moved a little closer to the nearest tube to get a better look, although he was careful to not actually touch it. The creatures inside were bipeds, but had especially skinny arms and legs covered in some kind of armor. Bernhard couldn't get a specific idea of what the aliens looked like, as they were all in helmets. Each one was taller than a human by about a foot on average, and there were objects floating next to them in the fluid that appeared to be weapons of some sort. For the most part, the weapons looked like spears, but there were things that were clearly triggers on the grips, implying that these could be used as more than just melee weapons.

This was clearly an army. And while Bernhard supposed there were reasons for an advanced alien civilization to send an army to Earth that didn't include invasion or war, he hadn't been sent up here with the directive of trying to figure out such possibilities.

He'd been sent here to see if the Visitor was dangerous. And now that he was certain it was, there was only one thing he was supposed to do.

"Okay, that's it," Bernhard said. "Mission's over. Everyone back to the *Ambassador*, on the double."

The military people, including Teng and his group, obeyed without question and left the room. Once they were back in the hallway, however, Bernhard found it wasn't quite so easy to get the science team to obey even these simple orders.

"What? No way," Dufresne when Bernhard repeated his command for the rest to hear. "Just like that, we're leaving? Bullshit. Come on, let us in there so we can see what the big bad captain is so squeamish about."

"Dufresne, don't," Johnson said, although she also looked

distinctly unhappy at this turn of events. "Bernhard's in charge, so we do what he says."

"Even when he's acting like a brainless dumbass?" Dufresne asked.

"Seriously, just tell us what's in there," Houston said.

"Alright, that's it," Bernhard said. "Sorensen, Stroebel, Hodges. Place the three American scientists under military arrest for interfering with an official government operation."

The three soldiers moved to do exactly as they were told without any further question. Houston put up his hands like he thought they might actually shoot him, while Dufresne just stood there with a shocked expression. Johnson was the only one who apparently still had her voice.

"Wait, what?" Johnson asked. "Bernhard, you can't be serious. I didn't even do anything!"

Truthfully, it was all a bit of bluff on Bernhard's part, anyway. He certainly had the power and authority in this situation to detain anyone not following orders, but he would never in a million years intentionally put any of the people in his command, civilians included, in spot where recklessness could harm them. The three scientists were no real threat, and he trusted his men enough to know they wouldn't take things too far. Really, Bernhard was just sick and tired of listening to them. They weren't contributing anything to this trip, and since this mission was more or less over now anyway, he had no qualms with sidelining them.

"Johnson, just do what I say, alright?" Bernhard turned to Teng. "I'm hoping that your side of the science team is going to be more cooperative?" The question came out a little more threatening than he had intended, and Teng gave him a long look before answering.

"All of my people will obey the orders I give them."

"Then order them to fall back to the *Ambassador*. There's a contingency plan that needs to be enacted."

Johnson shot him an angry, knowing glare. Bernhard did the best he could to not acknowledge it. Not yet at least. Everyone would know about the nuclear device once it blew up, but at least for the time being, it didn't appear that they would have to stay on the Visitor as it went off. Whatever the capabilities were of this alien army, they didn't appear to be awake yet. As long as they all hurried, Bernhard believed he could keep it that way.

Although there didn't seem to be any immediate reason to run, Bernhard still made them all move quickly back down the halls to the hangar. As they moved, Johnson, who had Hodges holding her tight by the arm with one hand while he kept his sidearm in the other to keep her in line, turned to Bernhard.

"Look, I understand that there's nothing we can do to stop this, but can't you at least tell us what you saw in there?"

"Gonna try to find one last detail that might change my mind, Doctor?" Bernhard asked.

"No, but I'm still the lead scientist here. At the very least, my position should give me the right to know what exactly it is that's going to make us give up all chance of studying this.

"It's an army, Johnson. Thousands of creatures that appear to be alien soldiers, and all of them in stasis."

"Well, if they're in stasis, what's the big deal?" Dufresne asked.

"The big deal, Dufresne, is that some advanced civilization sent a huge force of armed and armored troops all the way from some distant part of the galaxy to our planet. The fact that they're all asleep doesn't matter. Things that are asleep are meant to wake up eventually. If the Visitor contains more than just that one hall of soldiers, and I see no reason why there wouldn't be more, then them waking up and making their way planet-side could mean big trouble for humanity."

"Well, okay then," Johnson said.

Bernhard stopped. Everyone else stopped along with him. "That's it, Johnson?" he asked. "You're not going to try talking me out of it?"

"Talking him out of what, exactly?" Houston asked.

It took every ounce of Bernhard's control to keep a straight face and not curse. Given that he was going to set the nuclear device off one way or the other now, he supposed there was no reason to keep it a secret anymore. Still, he had just let it slip that there was a backup plan of some kind. Normally, he was better than such mistakes. Johnson, apparently, could bring them out in him.

"Teng, lead everyone back to the *Ambassador*," Bernhard said. "I need a moment to speak to Dr. Johnson alone."

Teng did as he was told, leaving Johnson and Bernhard alone in the hallway together. From the knowing and almost amused look on her face, Johnson knew exactly what he was thinking. "You can't blame me for that one. You let that little detail spill without my help."

"For the last time, Johnson, there's no detail to spill."

"Really? You're still sticking to the story?"

Bernhard sighed and put a hand to his face. "You are a pain in the ass, Johnson. You know that, right? So fine. There's a nuclear bomb on the *Ambassador*. You know it and I know it, and after I set it up on the Visitor, everyone else on the mission is going to know it, too. What bothers me is that you don't seem to be trying to stop me."

"Do you want me to stop you? News flash, but I'm not the one carrying the big honking rifle."

"You tried to talk me out of it before, and I fully expected you to try talking me out of it again."

"I already said my peace, Bernhard. Obviously, I'm not going to convince. I think you're making a serious mistake, but there's nothing I can do about it."

"You honestly still think blowing the Visitor up is a mistake knowing what it's here for?"

"Well, we don't know exactly what it's here for. We know it's carrying alien troops and yeah, that seems pretty bad. But you're the military mind here. Do you honestly mean to tell me that you can't think of a dozen reasons why blowing the Visitor up right now could cause problems?"

"I can think of plenty of reasons not to blow it up, alright? I've got a whole list in my head. But I also have one very good reason to want to get rid of this ship, and the God's honest truth is it has nothing to do with my orders."

Johnson looked taken aback by this. "Really? What is it?"

Bernhard turned and started marching back down the hall in the direction of the others. "You know what? It's none of your business. Now I suggest you follow me unless you want to end up as irradiated particles floating through space."

Back in the hanger, everyone had gathered around the *Ambassador*. Teng had formed up most of his people to form a perimeter around the shuttle, while the America military had taken up positions at the exit ramps. The two other American scientists were already on board. The Chinese scientists, however, were nowhere that Bernhard could see.

"Teng, where are the rest of your people?" Bernhard asked.

Teng, for the first time in the mission, tried to pull rank. "They are following my orders."

"And what were your orders?"

"They are need to know only, and you do not need to know."

Bernhard stopped and stared at him. He wasn't exactly surprised, yet he was still disappointed. "I'm the one who's been given command of this mission, so I would say that, yeah, I do in fact need to know."

He heard noises coming from behind him. He looked in the direction of the many boxes holding the alien fighter crafts to see one of Teng's soldiers coming back around it with the Chinese scientists.

"They're back, so it doesn't matter," Teng said.

Bernhard looked over at his rangers and Air Force spec ops people. All of them had their weapons in hand and ready, and there was a tension in them that showed they were prepared for a fight if it came to that. The question was, did Bernhard want to push this that far?

He cursed quietly to himself. It had been a mistake to let Teng out of his sight for any period of time. Of course, he would take advantage of the moment to get extra intel or material when Bernhard wasn't looking. Bernhard couldn't even blame him, because if the situation were reversed and Teng was the one in charge of the entire mission, Bernhard would have done the same. Anything to attempt to give his own country the advantage in whatever arms war the Visitor was going to start.

Bernhard reminded himself that, if the *Ambassador* did make it back to Earth in one piece, it would be landing at an American airbase. If Teng or any of his people had physically taken anything from the Visitor, it would get found and intercepted during their quarantine period after the mission. If all they had was knowledge, well, there was nothing Bernhard could do about that.

"Better get all your people on board and strapped in," Bernhard said tensely. Teng nodded, then motioned for them to follow him. As they filed on, Bernhard approached Zersky, Hodges, and McNeil.

"You three, I want you to get on board after them. Keep an eye on them and make sure nothing fishy happens. And no matter what happens next, do not, under any circumstances, allow them back out of their seats."

"Any circumstances at all, sir?" Hodges asked.

"That's correct. I'm sure you all understand my meaning?"

"Yes, sir!" all three of them said. They went on board, leaving Bernhard outside the craft with Johnson and the three rangers.

"Johnson, you better get on board as well."

"Aren't you going to need help with the bomb?" Johnson asked.

Hatch looked at the other two in confusion. "Bomb? What bomb?"

Bernhard gave Johnson the stink-eye. "Move, Johnson. Now."

Once she was back inside, Bernhard turned to the rangers again. "The bomb you three are going to help me unload. It's hidden in the cargo section. We're going to set a timer on it and leave. I trust that you will all remember your duty and follow my command, correct?"

The rangers all nodded their assent. This was more like it. Whether or not they approved, they didn't let their feelings show. They were simply going to do their duty without question.

They followed him up into the *Ambassador*. Everyone else in the shuttle stared after him as he ignored them all and instead made a beeline to the cargo hold. Once inside, he walked right up to where he had left the thermonuclear device at the ready.

It wasn't there.

CHAPTER SEVEN

He had the rangers guard the entrance to the hold while he did a thorough check of the entire area, just on the off chance that it had somehow simply shifted from its place while they'd been gone. But there weren't exactly many places in a space shuttle where a nuclear bomb could have slipped where no one could see it. The only possibility at all was that someone had intentionally moved or taken it.

Bernhard directed the rangers to get out of his way, then ordered everyone who had already strapped in to orderly depart the *Ambassador* and line up just outside the shuttle. Although his tone was the textbook example of measured calm, he could tell from the look on everyone else's face that they knew something was terribly, horribly wrong. Even Dufresne kept a tense silence as she went back down into the hangar and stood stiffly beside everyone else. Bernhard did his best during the whole thing to stay in a position where he could see every single other person, but considering how many there were, it was nearly impossible. Once they were all out and lined up, Bernhard stood in front of them and eyed them all.

"Bernhard, what's wrong?" Johnson asked.

"Not a single one of you is to speak unless I speak to you first, you got that?" Bernhard commanded. Johnson closed her mouth, but her eyes remained wide and trembling.

Okay, he had to stop and think here. He had somehow managed to misplace a nuclear weapon, but there weren't many possibilities. The way he saw it, all possible answers fell into one of two categories. The first was that someone among his group had done something with it. The second was that something else had come along while they were searching the Visitor and taken it. Under these circumstances on Earth, he would have first gone to look at any surveillance footage, but thanks to the peculiar properties of the Visitor, that simply wasn't going to happen here. He checked the time on his watch to find that less than an hour had passed between them first getting off the *Ambassador* and then getting back on again. For roughly twenty minutes of that, they had still been in the hangar within view of the shuttle, so nothing could have come during that time. It did leave plenty of time for something to show up, enter the shuttle, take the bomb, and then leave, but it wasn't like a nuclear weapon was light. It would probably take more than one person, or at least more than one human, to carry it. If multiple aliens had been in the hangar, there must be some way to tell, but they had yet to see any sign of anything alive on the ship that wasn't in stasis.

So that left the humans. Had there been enough time where anyone was out of his sight where they could have taken or at least moved the bomb somewhere he couldn't find it? Teng cleared his throat. "Bernhard, tell me what is happening."

Despite his best efforts at keeping a straight face, Bernhard sneered. "Sure, I'll go right ahead and do that once you tell me what your people were doing over by those box things."

"I already said, that is not something you need to know."

"Oh trust me, it is." Bernhard raised his rifle and pointed it in his direction. Instantly, every single person with a gun had it up and pointed at somebody, with the Chinese aiming at the Americans and vice versa.

"Whoa, whoa, whoa!" Johnson said. She ran right between Teng and Bernhard, putting herself directly in both of their lines of fire.

"Johnson, what the hell are you doing?" Bernhard asked.

"I was going to ask you the same question. Has everyone here suddenly gone insane?"

"It's gone, Johnson," Bernhard said. "Someone took it."

"What? How could that be possible?" she asked.

"What's gone?" Houston asked. Even though none of the weapons were aimed directly at him, he still had his hands up like he thought he was under arrest. "Could someone please explain to me why we're suddenly all lined up out here with freaking guns pointed at each other?"

Bernhard took a deep breath. This wasn't productive. "Teng, I'm going to lower my weapon and have every one of my people lower theirs. After your people do the same, I'll tell you what I can, but only if you do the same afterwards. I'm putting some faith in you here. Can I do that?"

After a moment's hesitation, Teng nodded.

"Alright. Lower your weapons."

On command, all of the Americans did as he said. A split second later, Teng and the Chinese followed suit.

"I was tasked with control over a nuclear device," Bernhard said after some hesitation. Honestly, at this point, there was zero reason to keep being secretive about it, and it was only paranoia that had driven him to suddenly raise his weapon. For all his thoughts earlier about needing the Americans and the Chinese on this mission to work together better, he had fallen into the same us-versus-them mentality.

Teng nodded. "I know."

Bernhard almost asked how, but again, if the situation were reversed, he was sure that he would have already poked around and found out as well. "I was instructed to use it to destroy the Visitor if we found anything at all that implied that it was a threat."

"Wait, you were just going to kill us all?" Dufresne asked.

"Not that I'm talking to you right now, Dufresne, but it's not like that was plan A. However, if had come down to our lives versus the lives of everyone down on Earth, the decision would have been easy."

"But now you're saying it's gone?" Li asked. "Have the Americans developed a nuclear weapon so small that someone can just walk off with it?"

"No, it's not small, but yes, it's gone," Bernhard said. "Either something on the Visitor came and took it, or else someone here with the group managed to make it disappear in the brief time where I wasn't watching them. So Teng, mind finally telling me what your people were doing over by those fighter crafts?"

Teng took a long moment to consider this, then nodded to his people. "Simple intelligence gathering. We were leaving, so I wanted our scientists to see the alien craft first. Even if they only saw it for a minute or two, that would give our government a potential advantage in the arms race that is to follow all this."

Johnson scoffed. "You make it sound like an arms race is inevitable, like every country in the world has already decided to use this as an opportunity to get ahead of the others rather than work together."

"Hate to break it to you, Johnson, but that's exactly what's already happened," Bernhard said.

Xiang, who had been listening to one of the other scientists translate all this for him, spoke up. Li interpreted for all the others. "He says it doesn't have to be like that, at least not between our countries. We are both here, so we should be able to share what we find."

Sorensen snorted.

"Do you have something to say, Sorensen?" Bernhard asked.

"Sorry, sir. I just think it's a pretty ironic thing for one of them to say, considering they weren't planning to share this information until they had guns against their heads."

"Stop with all this 'they' stuff," Johnson said. "We're all here together, so we're all the same side. There's no geopolitical boundaries up here."

Bernhard sighed. "She is right. Paranoia right now is only going to hurt us. We need to make a vow, right now, that we're going to share information, Teng. Because until that bomb is found, we most certainly aren't leaving."

"Do you honestly think someone here could have taken it?" Teng asked.

"While it's highly unlikely, it's not something we can rule out."

"Then I am telling you right now that none of my people had anything to do with this," Teng said. "My superiors already knew in advance that this was likely your plan, and I was instructed to help you carry it out, should it come to that."

"Just as long as you got as much extra intel as possible first, right?" Bernhard asked.

Teng shrugged. "That is not incorrect."

While Bernhard still wasn't sure how much he could trust Teng, or even if Teng could trust that no one among his own group had their own hidden agenda, the plain fact here was that it should have been practically impossible for Teng's people, even if they were all working together, to grab the nuclear weapon and hide it somewhere else without any on the American side being aware. While there still might not have been reason for the two groups to completely trust each other, logic made it likely that none of the humans were the culprit here.

Which only left the possibility that they weren't as alone in being awake on this ship as they thought.

"Whoever or whatever took the bomb, we have to find it," Bernhard said. "I'm sure a nuclear device is more like a kid's toy to aliens that can use all this other tech, but we still can't have it in enemy hands. That's our priority now."

"Are you still going to try to use it to blow up the Visitor?" Johnson asked.

"I can't give you a straight answer to that," Bernhard said.

"Can't, or won't?" Dufresne asked.

"Can't. The situation is rapidly evolving. If something else is alive and awake on this ship, then the danger to both us and Earth is worth than we were already thinking. All of you scientists were complaining about not being in on any of the thoughts and planning? Well, congratulations. You've got your wish. We need to find that bomb, and we're probably going to need to go deeper into the Visitor and learn its inner workings to do that."

It was notable, Bernhard thought, that none of the scientists seemed quite so enthusiastic about this as they had been before.

Finally, he realized, he'd found the perfect way to shut them up: give them exactly what they wanted and then let them realize all of this was more complicated than they expected it to be.

Bernhard motioned for them all to move out. They were going to start by thoroughly checking the hangar for the bomb and then, if they didn't find it, it was time to go deeper.

CHAPTER EIGHT

"I have to pee. Really," Dufresne said. Bernhard tried not to lose his cool. It was the sixth time she'd said that in the last ten minutes. So much for her being quiet.

"I wonder how aliens go to the bathroom?" Houston wondered out loud.

"Out of all the scientific problems you people could be working on in this place, that's the one you're fixating on?" Bernhard asked.

"Maybe it's just Dufresne's constant talking about it, but I feel like I need to as well," Johnson said.

Bernhard looked over at his and Teng's people to a number of them nodding in agreement. There was nothing he could do about biological needs, he supposed. He could probably do with such a break himself.

The problem was, it wasn't like there were any bathrooms around here. They had been wandering, making a map of the ship and its layout, all the time keeping an eye out for any sign of the bomb or whatever had taken it. So far, all they had managed to find was a number of long rooms just like the first one they'd discovered containing the alien troops in stasis. Each new room found, and the uncountable number of aliens trapped inside, cemented the idea in Bernhard that destroying all of this was the only way. The only difference between the rooms seemed to be the kind of soldiers they contained. Although he knew he couldn't make assumptions about alien military tactics, there seemed to be infantry, shock troops, pilots, and maybe even the alien equivalent of special forces. And still, through all of it, they still hadn't been able to find any explanation on what, exactly, the aliens wanted to do by coming to Earth.

"As weird as it's going to be," Bernhard said, "I guess we

don't have any choice but to designate some random section of hallway as the place where we're going to relieve ourselves."

Li spoke up. "Are we going to be allowed to have privacy for this, or are you going to be watching all of us like you don't even trust us then?"

Dufresne held up her hands. "Bernhard, I don't care what you say, but I not going to let you watch as I —"

"Nobody's going to watch anything, okay? Jesus." Bernhard found a short side hall that didn't seem to go anywhere but directly into a wall for no apparent reason. As messy as it would end up being, that was the best they could do for privacy on such notice. "Okay, so this is the designated restroom. One person at a time, and everyone else is going to take a few minutes to rest out here while we wait. Dufresne, you go first."

"Actually being nice to me for once, Bernhard?" Dufresne asked.

"No, I just want you to shut the hell up about your bladder."

While the all lined up in the main hall for their turn, Bernhard took his place at the back of the line and sat on the floor with his back against the wall. He kept his rifle ready just in case anything changed, but otherwise, he let himself rest. He hadn't realized until now just how tired he was, but there wouldn't be any opportunity for true rest anytime soon. As long as there was any possibility that they weren't alone on the ship, he had to remain vigilant.

"Bernhard?" Johnson asked. He jumped at her voice. He didn't even realize until he opened his eyes that he'd passed out for just a moment, and in the meantime, Johnson had found a seat next to him. So much for remaining vigilant.

"Johnson, is there something I can help you with?"

"I was just coming to see how you were doing. You look like your nerves are frayed."

"They're not frayed. I've had more stressful missions than this."

"I also wanted to ask you about something you said earlier."

Bernhard sighed. "If this is about my reasons for doing this, I told you that it's none of your business. I let slip something personal that I didn't mean to, and I would appreciate it if you just let it go."

Johnson looked away from him. "Maybe I should. But I also have to wonder it, whatever it is, it's affecting your judgment."

"I passed all the requisite psych tests, which is more than I can say about a couple of the other people here."

"Is it a family member?"

"Johnson, seriously, why can't you let this go?"

"Because you seem to be isolating yourself. And as lead scientist on the American side, I think I should have some say in whether or not that can put us in jeopardy."

They finally looked at each other. While she was certainly pretty and fascinating, he didn't want to get too close to her. There'd once been a time when he hadn't had any connections to others at all, and that had allowed him to keep a purely military-related approach to all problems. Anything he did either served his country, or it didn't. But that had changed a little over four years ago.

"I have a daughter," he said to her, keeping his voice low enough that this particular tidbit of information stayed between the two of them.

Johnson smiled, then thought about it. "But not a wife or girlfriend?"

"Her mother was also Air Force. We let off some steam together as a one-night thing. There was nothing particular between us, but nine months later, Victoria came along."

"How old is she?"

"Um, I think she just had her fourth birthday?"

"You think? You don't know?"

"No, I don't. I rarely see her. After Victoria was born, her mother decided to leave the Air Force and works now as a private contractor in Florida, while I'm still based in Nevada."

"So she's not really in your life very often?"

"No."

"But she's still important enough to you that you think about her."

"More than think, Johnson. There's no animosity between me and her mother at all, and she has a husband now that loves my daughter very much. But even though I'm not there and can't ever be there, given how much I've dedicated myself to my military career, I do everything I can to have some kind of presence in her life. Sometimes I'm not so good at it, but I pay my child support every month and then some. There's already enough money in the bank for her to go to a smaller college after she graduates high school, and I'm still putting money in. But although she knows I exist, sometimes I think she wouldn't even recognize me if she saw me."

"I'm sorry."

"Don't be. I'm not exactly father material. Her mother and stepfather will give her a good life. All I can do is make sure she survives long enough to have that life."

"But, Bernhard, that doesn't mean you have to be suicidal destroying the Visitor."

"I'm willing to die if I have to if it keeps her safe, but that's far from the first option. However, if at any point I come to the conclusion that it's a matter of her life versus mine, even if there's only a slight chance at her getting her, then I won't hesitate. And I won't let anyone else stop me, either."

"Hmm," Johnson said quietly. She got a far-away look in her eye. Bernhard cocked an eyebrow.

"Now you're the one that looks like she has something on her mind that might affect her judgment."

"Huh? Oh, no, you don't have to worry about that. I was just...thinking."

"About?"

"It's personal."

Bernhard stared at her unblinkingly until she realized the irony in her trying to use that excuse. She chuckled.

"Okay, fair enough, but I'm sure you've already got a detailed file on me."

"Even the most detailed file is only going to be facts. It's not going to include your emotions."

Johnson nodded but stayed silent for a while. Bernhard thought maybe the conversation was over when she finally spoke up. "It's just that all your talk of your kid made me think of mine."

Bernhard tried not to act surprised. "I guess the file on you isn't as detailed as it should be. I didn't say anything about you having a child."

"That's because I don't," she said quietly. "I was going to, but it didn't happen."

Bernhard waited, knowing that pushing her was the wrong tact to take right now.

"I got pregnant in high school. Junior year. But when I got to eight months, um, he didn't make it."

"I'm sorry, Johnson."

"I threw myself completely into school after that, and my grades became the best they've ever been. They stayed that way through college, too. I guess you could say that's how I got to be where I am. Now, I don't actually want any kids. I love my career and don't have much time for anyone else. But I do think of him sometimes. Sam. I was going to name him Samuel. And while he wasn't expected, I was prepared to love him and do everything in my power for him. So, I guess what I'm saying is that I think I get it. I may not have or want children of my own, but I understand that need."

Bernhard nodded. He wasn't sure what to say after that, but thankfully, he didn't have to.

"Dr. Johnson, your turn in line if you need it," Hodges said.

"Boy, do I ever," Johnson said. She got up without any further glance at Bernhard so she could take her turn in their makeshift bathroom. Once she came back, it was Bernhard's turn.

Doing his best *not* to pay attention to anything else in the hall other than what he was doing, Bernhard did his business quickly, zipped back up, and then, given the privacy of where he was for the moment, stopped to consider the situation. The Visitor was enormous, and it would be ridiculously difficult for them to search the entire thing for the bomb. Instead of wandering around aimlessly, they needed to find some kind of central control area. A ship this advanced had to have a way to track people and things aboard it. That way, too, the scientists might be satisfied if they got access to some form of alien computer.

Still, despite the likelihood that the bomb had been taken by something from the Visitor itself, he couldn't escape the nagging feeling of paranoia that someone from their group still might be the culprit. The problem with that idea, though, was motive. Sure, there were people among his team that would have a reason to either steal or hide the bomb, but what would be the point in the long run? He felt like he was missing something, something important.

"Captain?" Bernhard turned at the sound of the voice to see Stroebel in the short hall with him. "Is everything okay?"

"Yeah," Bernhard said. "I was just thinking. What is it?"

Stroebel looked over his shoulder in the general direction of where the others would be around the corner. "I wanted to talk to you. In private."

Bernhard stood straighter. "What is it? Is something the matter?"

Stroebel walked up to him. In fact, he stood much closer to Bernhard that he was comfortable with. He looked down for a second as though he were considering exactly how he wanted to word what he was going to say. Then he looked back up at Bernhard and opened his mouth.

He spit at Bernhard, but the things coming out of his mouth were not saliva.

Bernhard reacted quickly, his nerves already on edge thanks to the direction of his thoughts and Stroebel's proximity. He dropped down just in time to avoid whatever Stroebel ejected from his mouth and felt moisture graze his hair as it arced over him. It made a strange buzzing sound, something like a mosquito, and

Bernhard's short-term memory told him that was an important detail, that he'd heard something about a noise like that recently, but he didn't have time to think about it. Instead, he immediately went for a throat punch on Stroebel. Stroebel's reflexes were fast, but he hadn't been expecting a counter-attack, and despite backing away, he still caught much of Bernhard's force in his neck. As Stroebel staggered and then fell onto his back, Bernhard grabbed his rifle from where he'd set it against the wall and turned it onto Stroebel.

"Listen up, Ranger. You have exactly five seconds to explain to me what the hell you're doing."

Stroebel looked like maybe he was trying to answer, but Bernhard's punch had made it hard for him to breathe and he choked as he tried to find words. Bernhard heard several others in the outer hall respond to the sounds of a scuffle, but before they could get here, Bernhard heard that insectoid buzzing again from behind him. He turned, unsure what to expect.

The glob Stroebel had spit at him had hit the wall and slid to the floor. Now, covered in mucus, the glob unfolded from itself to show a mass of three worms. Each worm, once it was separated from the others, was about one foot long with a tiny maw full of sharp teeth at one end. At irregular intervals down their segments, the worms each had three bulbous pink areas that pulsed like hearts. They seemed disoriented by their unexpected trip into the wall, but they quickly oriented themselves and turned to Bernhard.

Zersky was the first one around the corner. "Bernhard, are you okay? Stroebel, what are you...oh holy hell!" Zersky saw the worms and aimed his weapon. Before he could pull the trigger, the worms dashed forward with unbelievable speed. Two of them rushed right past Bernhard. He didn't have any time to figure out where they went, as the third coiled up and then sprang directly for Bernhard's face. He raised his weapon in an attempt to slap the creature away, except the worm immediately wrapped around his rifle and squeezed tight. The lightweight but strong polymers that made up the rifle should have been able to stand up to the force, but the worm crushed the rifle in a matter of seconds and then was once again coming for Bernhard's face. He dropped the weapon and grabbed for the worm, catching it right as the toothed mouth tried to get between Bernhard's lips. He lost his balance in the struggle and fell backward, hitting the floor hard enough that his vision flashed white.

Elsewhere nearby, Bernhard could hear multiple shouts and screams, as well as clear noises of a struggle as others on the team must have been fighting off the two other worms. Someone fired multiple shots, and someone else – possibly Dufresne – was screaming for help to get one of the creatures off of her. Bernhard, unfortunately, couldn't pay attention to any of that. It took all his strength and concentration to keep the worm from making any progress on him. It had given up on getting into his mouth, apparently, and was instead snapping at his nostrils. Bernhard had absolutely no clue what this thing was, but if it desperately wanted to get inside him, then he desperately wanted to keep it out.

Teng ran into Bernhard's field of vision and knelt down to help wrestle the worm away. With the combined strength of both of them, Bernhard was finally able to get the thing away from his face.

"Hold it still on the floor!" Teng said. Bernhard did his best, but the thing was slippery and strong. Whatever Teng planned on doing, he needed to do it fast or else the worm would literally slip right through Bernhard's fingers and go after another target. Teng disappeared out of sight for just a second and reappeared with his own rifle. Holding the rifle butt down, Teng smashed directly onto one of the worm's pink bulbs. The bulb splattered, breaking the worm in two.

The two halves wriggling in Bernhard's hands kept moving for nearly half a minute before they finally fell still. Bernhard wondered for a moment if they were like certain other worms, where the two halves might grow to create two whole new worms, then watched with relief as the two parts instead shriveled and dried up.

Finally, satisfied that the worm wasn't going to somehow pop back to life and come after him again, Bernhard let go and turned to face the others.

All the members of their team had gathered at the end of the short hall, crowding around to see just what the hell had happened. The scientists had stayed back up to this point, with the military members coming forward and preparing to fire at whatever bizarre alien threat might come at them. Bernhard saw the second of the three worms on the floor nearby, also with one of its bulbous pink nodules crushed.

"Where'd the third one go?" Bernhard asked.

One of the Chinese scientists said something that Teng translated. "He says he saw it going down the hallway. There's no telling how far it went or how fast."

"Would someone please mind telling me what the hell that was?" Hodges asked.

"I don't know," Bernhard said, then pointed at Stroebel where he was still sprawled out on the floor and trying to catch his breath. "But he might."

CHAPTER NINE

Among their military equipment, they had some heavy-duty zip ties, which they immediately used to bind Stroebel's hands behind his back while Bernhard told the others exactly what he had just seen.

"He spit at you?" Houston asked. "He spit *worms* at you?"

"Sure did," Bernhard said. "Johnson, you're our biologist. Teng, who's yours?"

Teng ushered one of the Chinese scientists forward and introduced him as Pai. Bernhard recognized him as the member of their team that would have been grounded for his mild asthma if the Chinese hadn't pulled their bureaucratic weight to ensure he stayed on the team. Now, Bernhard supposed, was the moment where the guy would get to prove he was as important as they said it was.

"Johnson and Pai," Bernhard said. "You two gather up the remains of those worms. All military, keep an eye on Stroebel. We're going to move this whole party to somewhere we can have a nice chat with him."

They passed a few more of the rooms full of sleeping soldiers before Bernhard found something different that might suit their needs. This room had a series of long tables in it, although there was nothing on them and absolutely no other furniture or decoration that Bernhard could see. The tables would make for a good place for the scientist to study their specimens while the military side was forced to conduct an interrogation of one of their own.

Stroebel was forced to sit on the floor next to the wall while the rest of the military contingent surrounded him. Most of them kept their weapons at the ready. Although Bernhard didn't want to believe that one of the people under his command was some kind of traitor or spy or…whatever the hell he was, Bernhard couldn't deny what he'd seen with his own eyes.

And already, before he even started questioning the man, he wondered if Stroebel was the only one like this.

"First, tell us who or what you are," Bernhard said. When Stroebel began to open his mouth, Bernhard held up his hand to stop him. "And don't get cutesy by giving me your name and rank. I want to know what you really are. And if anything tries to come out of your mouth this time other than words, then I will not hesitate to give the order to kill you."

All expression vanished from Stroebel's face. He simply cocked his head and stared blankly ahead of him. "Very well," Stroebel said in a monotone. "As the language of this one's kind would say it, this one's cover is blown. I do not see any particular reason to keep pretending. This might even make an interesting game to pass the time."

Bernhard exchanged looks with Teng before continuing. "Are you Stroebel, or are you something else pretending to be Stroebel?"

"I am the Nerve. But I believe what you really want to know is whether this one that you call Stroebel is alive. The answer is no, not in the capacity you would understand it."

Several of the people around him hissed in breaths at that, but Bernhard kept himself focused on the task. "When those worms came at me, they made a buzzing noise, like bugs. I knew something about that sounded familiar." Bernhard nodded at Sorensen. "When we went in to see the alien fighter craft, you said you heard something like that. Stroebel was standing right next to you, but he said he didn't hear anything." He looked back at Stroebel. "That was you, wasn't it?"

"That is correct, Captain Bernhard. Is there anything else you can deduce about me from what you already know?"

"One of those worms got to him and infected him somehow while we were all preoccupied with the craft," Sorensen said. "Is that what you're saying?"

"What exactly are those worms?" Bernhard asked.

"Those worms are me, and I am the Nerve."

"But what does that mean? How are you, this Nerve thing, related to the Visitor and why it's here?"

"The ship you refer to as the Visitor is my sheep, and I am the shepherd, protecting it from the wolves."

"Great," Zersky said. "It's talking in riddles."

"No, I think I get what it's trying to say," Bernhard said. "You're some kind of organic security system, aren't you?"

"That would not be a completely inaccurate way of looking at it."

"Sir," Sorensen asked, "how do we know anything it's telling us is true? It could be just feeding us a line of bullshit right now and we wouldn't know the difference."

"I am not programmed to continue lying after having been discovered," Stroebel, or more accurately the Nerve, said.

Sorensen clucked at that. "That's exactly what you would say if you *were* programmed to lie, isn't it?"

Stroebel shrugged, a movement made difficult by virtue of his hands still being tied behind his back. "That is a logical conundrum, is it not?"

"So are you saying that all those worms were you?"

"I am a hive organism, so yes."

Johnson came over to join them. "I just overheard that. Can I try asking him some questions?"

"Be my guest," Bernhard said.

"You took over Stroebel's body, but you said he was dead as far as we understand it," Johnson said. "What exactly do you mean by that?"

"I was forced to consume a portion of his brain when I entered him," the Nerve said. "Any individual that I take over effectively ceases to exist except as a part of me."

"And that's what you tried to do to me?" Bernhard asked. Despite himself, he found it difficult to keep the venom out of his voice.

"That is correct."

"Why?"

"Protocol for proper protection of the ship you refer to as the Visitor is take over all hostile invading forces that might potentially interfere with the Cortex's assignment."

"Who or what is the Cortex?" Johnson asked.

"You have already seen them."

"The army we saw in stasis," Bernhard said. "They're the Cortex? And what exactly is this assignment of theirs?"

Stroebel's next words came out in such a matter-of-fact fashion that it actually took a moment for Bernhard to truly comprehend the impact of what he was saying. "Eliminate or enslave all biological life forms on the planet you refer to as Earth."

Everyone stood there in absolute quiet for nearly half a minute. While Bernhard had known this was a possibility, maybe even the most probable answer, hearing it said in such a cold, simple way chilled his heart. "To what end?" Bernhard finally asked.

Interestingly, the Nerve, through Stroebel's facial expressions, showed its first emotion since revealing itself. It looked confused. "I do not understand the question."

"What do you mean, you don't understand?" Johnson asked. "Why would the Cortex want to kill everything on Earth?"

"Because that is what they are programmed to do. Just as I am programmed to do what I must to eliminate intruders on the Visitor. It is why they exist."

"But who programmed them?" Johnson asked. "Why would anyone possibly want that?"

"I do not understand the question."

Bernhard motioned for Johnson to stop asking questions.

Houston, however, had stopped any pretense of studying the desiccated worms and joined them. "You keep saying 'programmed.' But the worms appear to be biological, not some sort of robot. Same goes for all those troops we saw. I mean, it's not like we got a chance to study them up close, but from what little I got to see, they looked biological too."

"This is a peculiar assumption," the Nerve said. "Why must being programmed be separate from being biological? Does your species not have its own programming? Do you not sleep on a given schedule, seek out food, seek to mate and replicate yourselves? We are all following the functions that were given to us by our creators?"

"And just who created you?" Bernhard asked.

"I do not know, nor is it relevant. All that matters is the programming. The Cortex is programmed to devastate life. I am programmed to protect the Cortex."

"Okay, but then here's the million-dollar question," Houston said. "If the Cortex is here for the sole purpose of destroying all life on Earth, then why isn't it doing it? The Visitor has been in our orbit for over a week now. Why haven't they all just woken up so they can start raining fire and brimstone down on the planet?"

"Signal incomplete. Uplink failed."

Bernhard thought at first that the Nerve was saying something had gone wrong inside it. When it didn't say anything else, though, he began to understand.

"You're not saying that you're having a problem with some kind of signal. You're saying that's the reason the Cortex hasn't woken up."

"That is correct."

"I don't think I get it," Zersky said.

"I do," Johnson said. "The Nerve is a hive mind. It has multiple bodies in those worms, but they all share the same thoughts. And apparently, all the organisms on the ship are the same way. The Cortex is part of a hive mind as well…"

Bernhard nodded and finished the thought for her. "Except it's been cut off from the main portion of its intelligence. It's like one of us had our arm cut off. On every other level, the arm would still be us, but it's useless without the signal from our brain telling it to move or pick something up or shoot someone."

"That is not a totally accurate analogy," the Nerve said, "but it is close enough for your understanding. It is more correct than not."

"But that's idiotic," Houston said. "If we're dealing with an advanced alien race here, why would they send their shock troops to wipe us out knowing that they couldn't actually communicate with them and control them?"

"You just answered your own question," Bernhard said. "They obviously didn't know. The Visitor appeared in our skies, but then it ran into something it wasn't expecting."

Houston nodded, suddenly looking very deep in thought. "Maybe...maybe it has something to do with how bad our communications are screwed up while we're in here?"

"Whatever way it is that this hive mind of the Cortex communicates with its troops across light years, it works on some kind of wavelength that is getting interference from things on Earth," Johnson said.

"Things like our comm equipment?" Sorensen asked. "That can't be right. The Visitor is huge, and we didn't even arrive until today."

"It's not just us, but everything," Houston said. "We're floating above a planet with massive amounts of radio waves and cell phone signals and Wi-Fi signals..."

"Plus all the satellites we have in orbit," Bernhard said. He once again directed his words at the Nerve. "When the Cortex decided to send a group to wipe us out, they weren't paying attention to whether or not we were technologically advanced, were they? They just assumed that whatever we had, it wouldn't be enough. So there was no backup plan for waking the Cortex up when they got here."

"Again, you are more correct than not," the Nerve said.

"Wait," Zersky said. "You guys said this Nerve thing was just like the Cortex in the way they were connected. Why then are these worms able to communicate with each other when the Cortex can't?"

Most of them couldn't come up with an answer, but Houston

soon spoke up. "Something on the ship itself is jamming all the electronic signals. The Cortex that we saw in those stasis tubes are trying to communicate across space with all the chatter from Earth blocking them. But the Nerve is just trying to do it within the ship, so nothing is stopping it."

Bernhard found himself almost being grateful to Houston. Almost. "Is that all true?" he asked the Nerve.

"Again, you are –"

Bernhard interrupted. "More correct than not. Right, I've got the drill now, thank you."

"So what are we going to do with him?" Sorensen asked. "We can't just keep hauling him around with us. All it would take is him getting free at the wrong moment and we're all dead."

"If we keep you alive, can we trust you to behave?" Bernhard asked the Nerve.

"No. At my first opportunity, I will try to either kill you or turn you into another one of my bodies."

"Well, that was straightforward."

"As I told you, I am not programmed to lie after being discovered. Of course, that does not mean that I am not holding back certain information from you. Keeping quiet is not the same as lying."

"And yet you just volunteered that little tidbit to us. Why?"

"I may be an artificially constructed orgasm, but I still have a sense of fun. And I am going to enjoy watching all of you scramble about and turn on each other after I tell you that Stroebel is not the only one among your party that is infected with me."

Everyone tensed. Bernhard replayed the Nerve's words in his head, trying to make sense of exactly what he had just heard. His first inclination was to accuse the thing of lying, but already he had begun to accept the idea that the Nerve wouldn't lie, even if it did sometimes only give half-truths. Keeping his rifle at the ready, Bernhard turned to the others and looked at them all. Even the scientists who had been studying the worms were now gathered around. Those that didn't speak English listened intently as Teng translated for them everything the Nerve had just said. Bernhard watched for any signs or tells among them that they were the infected person the Nerve had mentioned, but there was nothing.

"Whichever ones of you it is, say so right now," Bernhard said. No one answered. It had been a long shot anyway, but Houston didn't seem happy with that.

"You said that once you were discovered, you couldn't lie," Houston said.

"No, the individual body hosting me will not lie once discovered. Any among you that are already secretly a part of me can continue with the subterfuge."

Sorensen raised his weapon and aimed it directly at Stroebel's head. "We should just blow this lying son of a bitch away."

Hatch put his hand on Sorensen's rifle, trying to direct it away from its target. "Sorensen, what the hell are you doing? That's Stroebel! You know, as in the guy who was grilling burgers with us in your backyard on Memorial Day? As in our friend?"

"You already heard him. That's not Stroebel anymore. Stroebel's gone, and now he's trying to turn us against each other."

The unfortunate truth, Bernhard knew, was that they had already been fully prepared to turn on each other long before this. Bernhard himself had been guilty of this. Now the Nerve was going to use their own insecurity and paranoia to rip them apart. He had no doubt that the Nerve was right, that there was at least one other person here who was no longer human, but if this went too far, then that insider wouldn't even have to do anything. They could all turn on each other based on arbitrary divisions – military versus scientists, Americans versus Chinese – and the Nerve wouldn't have to lift a single finger against them. Bernhard saw this, and he could stop it, but only if he kept his own distrusting nature in check. That was going to be easier said than done.

"Sorensen, lower your weapon," Bernhard said.

"Captain, if we don't kill it now –"

"Sorensen, if you do not lower your weapon in exactly three seconds, I am going to assume that your insubordination means that you are, in fact, infected by the Nerve and working to undermine us. And if I make that assumption, I will then assume that the only way to control you is to have every other person here open fire on you. One. Two…"

Sorensen snarled, but lowered his rifle.

"Stroebel stays alive for now. We might still be able to get some information from him. Meanwhile, this room is going to be our home for a while. No one leaves under any circumstances. Everyone stays within line of sight of everyone else. If anyone does anything to try to hide or break away from the group, that person will be assumed to be the Nerve and will be shot."

"So we're just supposed to stand around here doing nothing?" Hodges asked.

"No, all of you are going to stand around doing nothing." Bernhard went over to one of the table not being used to inspect the worms and pulled himself up to a sitting position on top of it. "Meanwhile, I'm going to sit right here and stare at all of you until I figure out which of you are actually the Nerve in disguise."

For the first time since being outed as the Nerve, Stroebel laughed. The sound was disturbing and unnatural coming from him.

"I will find this highly entertaining," the Nerve said. Then Stroebel slumped as if he had suddenly gone to sleep.

CHAPTER TEN

After several minutes of tense silence, Bernhard finally spoke.

"Every single one of you, disarm yourselves. Everything. Rifles, side arms, even any knives you might be carrying. Set them down carefully on the floor, and then go over to this far side of the room. Nobody make any sudden moves, and nobody get closer than two feet from any other person."

While the American military immediately started to disarm, Teng held up a hand indicating for his own people to not obey just yet. "Bernhard, how do any of us know that you're not the Nerve? You're keeping your own rifle ready, aren't you? This could just be a ploy to put us all in the perfect position to kill us."

"I guess you don't," Bernhard said. "But if any single one of us is going to survive this, there has to be at least one person completely above suspicion. If you all disarm and make yourself completely vulnerable to me yet I don't shoot, then those of you that aren't full of worms will know for certain that person is me."

"And if it isn't you?"

"Then everyone would die, but it isn't me. Despite the situation, none of us are going to get out of it if there isn't at least some trust."

Teng hesitated, then stooped to put his weapons on the floor. "I guess this means I trust you then," Teng said as he stood back up.

That's good, Bernhard thought. *Now comes the question of who do I trust?* The first thing he needed to figure out was if there was anyone in the group that he could be certain hadn't been taken over by the Nerve. Once everyone was in a position where he could see them, he started replaying the events of the last several hours in his mind. Unfortunately, there wasn't a single one of them that hadn't been out of his sight at least once. There was, however, at least one that had barely left his side as she was constantly pushing him to approach the mission in a less paranoid manner. He could think of three moments where Johnson had not been where he could see her. There had been when he'd led the group to look at the alien fighter craft, the moment she had been outside the *Ambassador* while he had searched for the nuke, and the moment where he had gone to relieve himself. The first two he thought were pretty easy to discount. She'd just been standing in the middle of the open hangar, and it seemed highly unlikely to him that a worm could have gotten to her there without anyone else noticing. The last instance, though, was a bit tougher. They all knew for a fact that at least one worm had escaped during the scuffle with the Nerve. Most people said they didn't have any clue where it had gone, and one had said they saw it escaping, but that could be misdirection. It was entirely possible that she'd been infected at that moment, although maybe not likely given that she had been at the far end of the line to start with when it all happened.

So he couldn't with one hundred percent accuracy say she was still who she said she was. But he had to have at least one other person he trusted, and in order to do that, he was going to have to overcome any natural inclination to distrust and instead take a leap of faith on someone.

"Johnson," he said. "You come join me." She looked a little surprised, but she wasted no time leaving the others and joining him.

"Does this mean you trust me?" she asked.

"Not yet. Not completely. I want you to pick up one of those guns at your feet and aim it at me."

She hesitated. "What? Why?"

"Just do it."

Cautiously, she bent down and took one of the rifles. She looked like she barely even knew how to hold it, but that could be an act. If she really was controlled by the Nerve now, and the Nerve shared all the information it got from individuals between all its bodies, then she would know exactly what to do with it.

Taking a deep breath and hoping his instincts weren't failing him, Bernhard turned his back to her.

"Bernhard? What are you doing?"

"If you're the Nerve, then this is your chance. You can kill me immediately, and then turn on the others and take most of them out before they could even move."

"Captain, are you out of your mind?" Zersky asked.

"No," Bernhard said. "But I have to take a risk somewhere, and this is where I'm doing it."

He closed his eyes for a moment, waiting for the bullets to enter his back and kill him. Instead, all he heard was a slight clatter as she put the rifle back on the ground. Smiling, he turned around to her.

"No, no. Pick that back up. I'm going to need you to keep it aimed and ready in case the actual Nerve suddenly decides to make a play."

"Except I'm not even sure how to shoot this thing."

"You pull the trigger. But please try not to unless I say so."

She picked it back up. As she moved, he couldn't help but notice the small smile at the corner of her lips that he'd put his faith in her.

Turning back to the group, he considered this time which ones he definitely could not eliminate as possibilities no matter what. The first among them were pretty much all the scientists on the Chinese side. Bernhard knew that Stroebel had been taken over in the box with the fighter, and since they had all gone off on Teng's command to look the fighters over, they had clearly been exposed along with Taam, the soldier that had accompanied them. Bernhard had them go over to a different wall from the others, all the while still keeping a close eye on them.

Next, Bernhard had to consider Teng. The most damning evidence that he might have been taken over at some point was that he'd sent so many of his people to a place where they themselves could have been infected. Then again, Bernhard knew exactly what it meant to put one's loyalties to their country ahead of all others, so the idea that Teng had only done it because he thought it would possibly put his country ahead of others in a future technology race wasn't far-fetched at all. There was also one major point in Teng's favor, considering he had in fact been the one to save Bernhard from the worm.

Then again, that could also have been a ploy to gain Bernhard's trust.

Bernhard made his decision. "Teng, get over here and take the rifle from Johnson." Teng nodded, and their eyes met for a moment in mutual respect. Once he had the weapon, Bernhard directed Johnson to get back to looking at the worm samples. They would need a more reliable method of detecting the Nerve that simply using Bernhard's best-educated guesses, and anything she could contribute to that goal would be necessary.

Next, there were the other two American scientists. They seemed like they were less likely to be possessed by worms purely because they had been with Johnson for most of the time, but there had been at least one moment where they hadn't been in Johnson's sight, the moment when Johnson had stayed behind to try to convince Bernhard not to use the bomb. It did seem unlikely that they were infected during that time, but Bernhard didn't want to risk it. Although, if he were being honest, he didn't want to give them a clear pass right now purely because of his dislike of Dufresne. The two of them were told to join Taam and the Chinese scientists. Dufresne, of course, protested up until she saw Teng's finger tighten on his trigger, after which she thankfully shut up.

And that left the majority of the military contingent. As much as Bernhard didn't want to do it, he immediately made Sorensen join the others. He'd been close enough to Stroebel to hear the whining noise as Stroebel had been infected, so he was also close enough that he could have been taken by a worm soon after. After some careful consideration, Bernhard had Zersky join Teng with a weapon. It was a calculated risk, but a plan was starting to form up in his head about how to finally ferret out the Nerve, and he needed more than one person with a gun in order to do it. He knew

Zersky well enough to say that he hadn't been acting at all unnatural, nor had there been many opportunities for him to be taken over.

"Teng, Zersky, both of you come over here," Bernhard said. He whispered his plan into their ears, doing his best to look as shady and untrusting of those remaining as he did so. It was important that those that he couldn't be sure of started to get nervous at this point. They both listened, and while Teng did not seem to approve, he did at least agree that there weren't many other ways to approach this at this point.

Teng took a moment to consider his own people, then directed three of them – Tshien, Ngai, and Yeow – to come over and join those with weapons, leaving Chow to join those that they couldn't be sure of. All that left then were Hatch, Hodges, and McNeil, all of whom Bernhard couldn't decide on one way or the other. To be safe, he had them join the larger group against the wall.

Altogether, there were seven that Bernhard believed he could trust not to be controlled by the Nerve, six of whom were military and knew how to handle a weapon. That would be more than enough for the highly distasteful thing he needed to do next. He reminded himself that this was a highly unusual situation with billions of lives in the balance, making this the only option.

The six members of the Chinese and American military with guns lined up in front of all the others. "I want you all to know that I only do this with the greatest reluctance," Bernhard said to the increasingly agitated group against the wall.

"Captain, what are you doing?" Hodges asked.

"I can't be certain whether any of you have been taken over by the Nerve," Bernhard responded. "And we cannot let the Nerve infiltrate us under any circumstances. The only choice we have is to kill you all."

"What?" Johnson screamed from her place at the table. "Bernhard, no! What the hell are you doing?"

"This potentially comes down to their lives versus the lives of everybody else on Earth," Bernhard said. "I told you I would do whatever it took to protect my daughter."

"But this is monstrous!" Dufresne yelled. "You won't be able to get away with this!"

"I'm sure some of you are still fully human," Bernhard said to the people against the wall. "And to you, I'm completely sorry. Teng, we're commanding our people to fire on three, understand?"

Teng nodded, and all six of them raised their rifles.

"One," Bernhard said.

"Bernhard, you can't!" Johnson said. "You say you're doing this for your daughter, then ask yourself if you'll ever be able to look her in the eye again if you do this!"

Bernhard ignored her. "Two."

Li started mumbling something to herself that might have been a prayer. McNeil made the sign of the cross over himself and looked upward as though to tell whomever he believed in that he would be coming soon. Dufresne just started screaming obscenities.

"Three."

Not a single one of them fired. But on the last number, four members of the group shoved the others forward, using the others as human shields as they tried to get out of the line of fire. Sorensen, Pai, Xiang, and Hatch all made a break for it, going directly for Stroebel all at once as they were one organism.

Which Bernhard knew, they were. There were three hidden pieces of the Nerve.

"That's them!" Bernhard yelled. "Take them out!" The six men with guns tracked the four trying to escape, but they moved faster than Bernhard would have expected. Whatever the worms eating away at their brains had done to them, they had also increased their speed and agility in a way that caught Bernhard completely off guard. He tried to fire at Sorensen as he leaped over the group, but the bullets did nothing but ping against the ceiling. Pai and Xiang went for Yeow and Zersky, the two of them trying to use Houston and Dufresne as meat shields. Yeow managed to get off a shot and hit Xiang in the chest, while Pai opened his mouth in preparation of spitting at Zersky. Tshien was close enough to whip his rifle around and use it as a club against Pai's back, causing the concentrated ball of alien worms that ejected from his mouth to fly over everyone's heads. Chaos reigned as those still remaining against the wall ducked, trying to protect themselves from the random bullets suddenly flying around the room. Hatch got off a lucky punch at Bernhard, ringing his bell for long enough that he dropped to his knees and had to shake his head to stop from seeing stars.

By the time Bernhard fully came back to his senses, Xiang was dead on the floor. Yeow, Ngai, and Teng were finishing off the worms from Pai's mouth before they could try to take over anyone. But most importantly, Pai, Hatch, Sorensen, Dufresne, and Stroebel were gone.

CHAPTER ELEVEN

Johnson slapped Bernhard across the face. He took it, accepting that he probably deserved it.

"You bastard!" Johnson yelled in his face. Her cheeks were wet from tears, but she had already stopped crying. Instead, her eyes were full of the fury of someone who had thoroughly fallen for a nasty bluff. "I actually thought you were going to kill them!"

"I may put my country and my daughter above everything else," Bernhard said as he rubbed the red mark on his jaw. "But I'm not so heartless that I would blatantly kill innocent people. I just needed the Nerve to think I would."

Houston picked himself up from where he'd been unceremoniously been thrown to the floor. "Wait a second," he asked. "Where the hell did Dufresne go?"

"They took her with them," Teng said. "There's no chance to save her. She is probably already part of the Nerve."

Bernhard saw several worms trying to work their way out of the mouth of Xiang's corpse. He had no choice but to smash the man's head with his rifle until he was certain that nothing else was going to come out. Once he was done, he finally had a chance to take stock of everything around them.

The room was a mess of bullets and casings and blood. None of their shots had actually gone into the walls, but whatever material they were made of had thankfully absorbed the impact and prevented ricochets. Chow, McNeil, and Hodges had already grabbed their weapons once more, while the weapons left behind by Hatch, Sorensen, and Stroebel were distributed among those scientists who had any experience at all with firearms. Li, the only one among the Chinese scientists that was still alive and human, stood where she had been against the wall, still too shell-shocked to move. Teng went over to her and gently coaxed her to join with

Johnson and Houston where they could continue examining the dead worms.

Johnson, however, wasn't quite finished with Bernhard yet. "That was a really shitty thing to do, you know."

"I said I was sorry," Bernhard said. "It was the only way I could think of that might smoke out the Nerve."

"So you were never really going to shoot them?"

"No."

"But what if it hadn't worked? What if you got to three and nobody had moved?"

"Then we wouldn't have been any worse off than we were before. It was a chance I needed to take."

"But how do you know for sure that the Nerve didn't leave one of its bodies behind to keep up the charade?" Houston asked. "There's still a possibility that someone among us could be an alien spy."

"Yes, it is possible," Bernhard said. "That's why we're not going to let our guard down anymore, and why we all stay within each other's sights at all times from now on."

"Where the hell did they even go?" Hodges asked. "You'd think the Nerve would stay behind to try killing us. I mean, it's not like it actually cares if it loses any bodies it takes over, right?"

"No, it probably doesn't," Bernhard said. "But as long as there are more of us than there are of it, the Nerve probably thinks it more tactically prudent to pull back rather than go kamikaze on us. Trust me, we haven't seen the last of them."

"So what are we going to do?" Houston asked.

"We need to get the hell out of here," Zersky said. "We should all get back on the *Ambassador* and head back to Earth. And as soon as we get out of range of whatever's messing with our communications, we send a message to Earth telling them to nuke the Visitor."

"That might be a good plan if I didn't suspect that the Nerve was already ahead of us," Bernhard said. "If it's not about to sabotage the *Ambassador*, then at the very least we could expect some kind of ambush before we got there."

"Then we need to find the bomb and set it off," Johnson said.

Bernhard gave her a curious look.

"What?" Johnson asked. "All hypotheticals are gone. We know exactly what alien civilization sent the Visitor and why. Maybe we could still try to salvage some tech from it, but there's no more chance of this just being E.T. wanting to borrow our cell phones for a call home."

"I must respectfully disagree," Teng said. "This is now about more than countries involved in petty squabbles. We need to do everything we can to keep the Visitor in one piece. Because all of Earth is now going to have to fight against an alien civilization."

"Well duh, not if we blow the aliens up first," McNeil said.

"No, Teng's right," Bernhard said. "Destroying the Visitor will only destroy those drones of the Cortex that are on this ship. As an alien race, they'll still be out there, and it will only be a matter of time before they send something to check why they've lost contact. When they do, we'll be facing them all over again, and this time probably with them having a way to speak to their hive mind despite our technology getting in the way. The only way the human race can be prepared against that is for us to harness any and all technology we can find on the ship to use against them. As of this moment, I am officially removing the destruction of the Visitor from our list of possible plays."

Johnson made a humorless chuckle. "Well, that's certainly turning the table a hundred and eighty degrees. I get what you're saying, Bernhard, but the bigger threat to the human race right now isn't the Cortex. It's the Nerve. If that thing were to get down to Earth and start taking over people..."

"It wouldn't get far," Bernhard said. "If the Cortex can't function right now on or near our planet, then neither can the Nerve. The only reason it's able to try picking us off in here is because there's something blocking our own communications. If we can find what that is and turn it off..."

Finally, Johnson looked like she was coming around to his

thinking. "Then the Nerve is no longer a hive organism. It's just a bunch of worms cut off from each other."

Bernhard nodded. "Worst-case scenario, the Nerve would still be able to replicate inside a host, but anyone it takes over would just be a brainless zombie. Best-case scenario, the Nerve would react in exactly the same way as the Cortex and shut down completely."

"All of that relies on something we still haven't accomplished yet," Li said. "We would need to find some kind of central control area of the Visitor. Then we would need to figure out how to operate the alien technology in order to turn it off."

"But what about the bomb?" Houston asked. "Aren't we still going to need to find it?"

"Maybe, maybe not," Bernhard said. "Even if, tactically, the best play the Nerve could do right now is to destroy the entire Visitor just so we can't get back to Earth to warn everyone about what we know, it wouldn't. You heard it. Its primary reason for existing is to protect the Visitor and everything on it from us. Blowing the ship up would be the exact opposite of its programming."

"There's still the question of what happened to the bomb in the first place," Hodges said. "If the Nerve is the life form on the ship that's working other than us, then how did it get into the *Ambassador* and walk away with a thermonuclear weapon? Can you imagine how many of those little worms it would take to do that?"

"What if the answer is related to something else we have been seeing?" Li asked.

Bernhard raised an eyebrow. "What do you mean?"

"The lack of radiation on any level whatsoever."

"Hey, yeah," Houston said. "It can't be a coincidence that we find the Visitor resists any and all signs of trace radiation, and then at the same time the device we brought that capable of large amounts of radiation just suddenly disappears."

"I admit that's an interesting coincidence," Bernhard said,

"but what would the connection be?"

Houston shrugged. Li and Johnson seemed equally baffled.

"Then I suppose that's something we'll need to remember but put on the back burner for now," Bernhard said. "Our number one priority for the moment needs to be taking down the Nerve. If we can accomplish that, then we can turn our attention to getting back to Earth and warning the world about what we've found out."

"We're going to still run into the same problem we've had up until this point," Teng said. "The Visitor is very large. We could very well search it for days or even weeks without finding the way to stop the jamming."

"And even though they don't have any weapons, there's still the Nerve's various bodies out there looking for the best way to kill us all," Hodges said. "Not to mention the worms, which could be anywhere at all on the ship and we wouldn't have any idea."

Bernhard put his head in his hands, rubbing his temples as though trying to hold back a headache. That was indeed a problem, and one he had no solution for at the moment.

"If only I had some Ozzy," he muttered.

"What was that?" Johnson asked.

"Ozzy Osbourne. I do my best thinking with music, but I couldn't exactly bring my MP3 player with me on my trip to a mysterious alien spaceship, could I?"

"The Sabbath years, or his solo stuff?" Johnson asked with a strange amount of enthusiasm.

Bernhard waved her off. "Just forget it. If anyone has any suggestions regarding an easy way to find some kind of control room, I'm all ears."

Everyone was silent.

"I was afraid of that," Bernhard said. "In that case, it looks like we're back to our original plan: wandering aimlessly until we find something interesting. Everybody pack up and get ready to move out."

CHAPTER TWELVE

An hour later, they were all tired, exhausted, and hungry. They didn't yet find a control room, but they did at least find something other than more rooms full of the Cortex trapped in stasis. The endless doors and inexplicable rooms finally yielded to a much larger archway. They approached it cautiously, but Bernhard could tell by the postures of the military folks that they desperately needed to find some place to stop and get a solid rest.

The massive room beyond the archway would not be it.

Bernhard repressed the urge to whistle in appreciation as they passed into the room, except *room* was a terrible word for it. Even calling it a hangar like the very first room they'd been in wouldn't correctly express the sheer size. *Cavern* wouldn't even work. Given that Bernhard had trouble seeing the ceiling through some kind of hazy wisps that might have actually been clouds, he hesitated even to call it a room at all. If they had been on Earth, he would have thoroughly believed they were out in the open.

"This...this is amazing," Houston whispered reverently. "This room must take up the largest portion of the ship."

"Maybe," Bernhard said. "Although we shouldn't make assumptions." He was hedging. In truth, he figured that Houston was probably right. The Visitor had certainly been massive, but the perspective in here almost made it look like it was larger in here than even on the outside. Hell, given that alien technology was involved, for all he knew, it really might be bigger on the inside.

"Maybe it's like the TARDIS," Johnson said.

"I have no idea what that means," Bernhard said.

"Wait, seriously?" Johnson asked. "How can you not know that?"

"Yeah, Bernhard," McNeil said. "Even I know about *Doctor Who*, and I hate television."

"Well, excuse me if I'm usually too busy defending liberty and such to pay any attention to pop culture," Bernhard said. Beyond its size, there was quite a number of things within the room to catch the eye. The sky, if it could really be called that, was a hazy red color, and the ground covered in some kind of purplish dirt. The land, such as it was, looked hilly, and appeared to go on for actual miles in most directions. All of this might have otherwise made this place the ideal spot for them all to stop and get some sleep, except immediately around them they seemed to be surrounded by something that Bernhard couldn't help but think of as an alien military base. There were buildings that were several stories tall (*actual buildings inside a room*, Bernhard thought with awe), but the architecture was unlike anything that could possibly be seen on Earth. In fact, the architecture seemed very off in relation to the simple geometric shapes and patterns that had seen everywhere else on the Visitor. They looked organic, like something an insect would build, but on a much larger scale. The entire area was surrounded by a fence, and just beyond was a long flat field. It was the items lined up in orderly rows in that field, however, that really inspired the most boyish parts of Bernhard's imagination.

"Oh my God," Bernhard said. "Are those what I think they are?"

"Depends," Houston said with something in his voice that might have actually been glee. "If you think those are fricking giant robotic mechs, then yeah, I think they are."

Calling them giant was something of a misnomer considering the scale of the rest of the room, but each one of the mechs was somewhere between fifteen and twenty feet tall. Their make and aesthetic implied the same designers as the buildings, yet they were very clearly made to resemble something vaguely humanoid, if again vaguely bug-like. Bernhard carefully approached the nearest one and inspected some of the details. There appeared to be handholds, although definitely not designed for human hands, that led up into something resembling a cockpit. Through the clear material at the front of the cockpit, he could see a complicated series of controls and possibly a chair or seat of some sort. The mech's arms had protrusions on it that were probably guns of some sort, as well as what looked to be a long, strangely shaped blade that could retract into the arm.

Basically, if someone had given the eleven-year-old version of Bernhard a pencil and paper, then instructed him to create a weapon called "The Badass Weapon of Pure Fricking Awesome," his adolescent self probably would have drawn something that looked exactly like this. Based on the number of orderly rows of the machines that he could see, Bernhard did some rough numbers in his head and came up with a rough estimate of about one hundred and thirty of the machines.

While normally that number might have been impressive, the adult tactical part of his brain immediately registered a problem. "That's not enough of these things."

"I don't know, Bernhard," Hodges said. "It looks like enough firepower to cause some serious damage to me."

"But it's out of proportion to the number of Cortex drones that we've been seeing," Bernhard said.

"I do not think the Cortex made these," Li said.

"I think you're right," Bernhard said. "But again, that doesn't make any sense. What would all these things be doing here if they were made or designed by a different civilization or alien race." As soon as he said it, a thought occurred to him. "Wait, I think I've got an idea. Everyone, follow me."

Bernhard led them away from the fenced-in area and to the nearest hill. The arrangement of the hills, with their squarish pattern around the peculiar base, brought to Bernhard's mind what the world looked like when flying above the Heartland states, and how the divisions between developed land always looked like perfect squares from the sky. As they got to the top of the hill and looked down beyond, Bernhard felt like his suspicions were confirmed.

Down in the valley between the hills, there was a very similar setup to what they had just seen. There was a selection of buildings, these one mostly round domes in shape, and several lines of what looked like might happen if someone crossed a crab with a tank. Everything from the coloring to the design clearly implied a very different designer than what they had already seen.

"Those are pretty cool, too," Houston said. "But I still don't get what we're seeing."

"I do," Bernhard said. "What do you want to bet somewhere in this room there's a square of land that's empty and waiting to be filled?"

"Filled with what?" Hodges asked.

Zersky answered before Bernhard could. "Us. There's a patch of land with humanity's name on it. And once the Cortex is finished with their complete extermination of us, our buildings and our weapons will go there."

Bernhard nodded. "We're in a trophy room. These are the alien cultures and civilizations that the Cortex have already wiped out."

Further inspection not only showed them that there were plenty more vanquished races among the Cortex's conquests, but that the air was full of them as well, far more than any of them suspected would have been possible. High up in various corners of the sky, there were floating buildings and vehicles that none of them could hope to reach at the moment, all of them bobbing in the air with no indication of how they had gotten there or what might be keeping them afloat.

The one thing they didn't find among this graveyard of civilizations, though, was anything alive. Even a few cursory inspections of the buildings failed to give them more than a vague idea of what the aliens who had once lived there had looked like. All other sign of their existence was gone, leaving the humans to make guesses at what they may have been like in the same way that paleontologists had to guess the skin color of dinosaurs.

"This is all very creepy," Johnson said. "I'm not sure if I want to stay in here for much longer."

"Really?" Bernhard asked her. "With all the scientific knowledge you could gain from studying all this?"

"Scientific knowledge can be gained by digging up the bones in a cemetery," Johnson said. "That doesn't make it feel any less ghoulish when you're going through it."

"I must agree," Teng said. "While the amount that could be learned here is staggering, wandering around dead alien worlds is not getting us any closer to shutting down the Nerve."

Teng was right, although Bernhard wasn't ready to admit it out loud yet. If this room showed them anything, it was that the Visitor was more vast than they had previously expected with surprising information that would take enormous teams of soldiers and scientists years to properly catalogue. Maybe the best course of action was, in fact, to head back to the *Ambassador* so they could get free of the jamming and report everything they'd seen and heard. And while the Nerve would surely be waiting for them there, they at least had an idea of what they were up against if they went back that direction. If they continued forward, however, they didn't even have a guarantee that it would provide them with a way to shut down the jamming or stop the Nerve. Tactically, a temporary retreat from the Visitor was seeming more and more like the most intelligent option.

"Alright. Here's what we're going to do," Bernhard said. "First, we need to find a defensible position where we'll be able to fight off the Nerve when it comes for us again."

"Don't you mean 'if' it comes for us again?" Houston asked.

"No, I don't. Maybe we can't be one hundred percent sure that it was telling us the whole truth earlier, but I do believe this much: it's going to do everything it can to get rid of us. Once we have this position, we need a solid rest. We'll take shifts sleeping so that —"

"Wait," Johnson said, holding up her hand and looking back over her shoulder. "Did anyone else hear that?"

Bernhard motioned for everyone to be quiet. For several seconds, he didn't hear anything. When he did, though, he recognized the sound immediately.

"It's Dufresne," Bernhard said. "It sounds like she's calling for help."

CHAPTER THIRTEEN

"Where is it coming from?" Teng asked. "It is hard to tell the direction of sound in this place."

Bernhard agreed. Although there was an enormous wall within easy walking distance of their current position, the room still felt like it was open air. There was even a slight breeze. The damned room was so large, it even had its own air currents. And yet there was a peculiar echoing quality to everything they said and heard.

"I think it's coming from that direction," McNeil said, motioning his rifle at a space further down the wall. It was difficult to judge how far they had already traveled, but if it wasn't for the difference in the architecture of the trophy buildings up ahead, Bernhard would have thought that the archway he saw looming there was the same one they had come in. That was apparently their way out of here for now, but if they had to come back here, they would need to be conscious of how easy it was to get disoriented in here.

They all approached the archway ready for combat, but as they went through, they didn't immediately see the source of any noise.

"Maybe we got the direction wrong," Teng said.

"Or maybe we were just hearing things," McNeil said.

"No, that was definitely Dufresne," Houston said.

"If it was, then we're probably about to walk into a trap," Bernhard said. "There's no reason why the Nerve wouldn't take her over right away. There wouldn't be a tactical advantage to leaving her uninfected."

"Sure there would be," Hodges said. "Leave her uninfected and she can be used as bait."

"She can be used as bait even if she already has a worm in her," Bernhard said. "As long as she hasn't been revealed definitively to be taken over, then she could continue to deny it right up until the moment one of us lets our guard down and she spits worms in our face."

"In that case, maybe the best plan of action would be to ignore any cries of help from her," Zersky said. Houston immediately balked.

"We can't do that! If there's any chance at all that she's uninfected, then we have to try saving her!"

"Houston, think about the stakes involved," Johnson said. "The likelihood of her being uninfected is so low that it practically doesn't exist. But there are billions of people on Earth who are counting on us. We have to weigh the options."

"Well, you know what?" Houston asked. He hefted the rifle he had picked up back in the room where they'd almost been executed. "Last I checked, I'm not military, so I don't have to follow the military commands. And I'm going to look for her. If the rest of you want to go forward and save the world instead of her, then be my guest."

Bernhard looked at Houston with renewed interest. He'd been so worried about his own concerns for the mission that he had completely missed it, but now it was painfully obvious. Houston was in love with Dufresne, or at least had some deeper level of feelings for her. Trying to convince him to ignore any further cries of help they might here wouldn't work. Houston would go off on his own at some point if Bernhard wasn't careful, and in the process, he himself would either get taken by the Nerve or else killed. As much as he'd rather not do it, it would save Bernhard a lot of headaches if they found Dufresne sooner rather than later and resolved this.

"Fine," Bernhard said. "If we hear her again, we go looking for her. But if we don't, we keep on going with our original plan of walking around aimlessly like a bunch of idiots."

Johnson raised an eyebrow at that. "Losing a bit of hope, Bernhard?"

"No. Now come on, everyone. This hall doesn't look quite the same as the ones we were in earlier."

Indeed, unlike the ones they had previously seen, these walls seemed to be made of a darker material, and every so often, they pulsed irregularly with a faint glow. Li took out her instruments and did a few of the same tests she had earlier. "I think we may be getting closer to some kind of power source," she said.

"Are you sure?" Bernhard asked. "To me, it just looks like we're going back in the general direction from which we came."

"No, I am not sure. Given the number of oddities about the ship, I would not be surprised at all if are in fact getting closer to whatever might be considered the heart of the Visitor."

Houston shrugged. "We've already got the Nerve and the Cortex. It wouldn't surprise me at all if there was in fact something on this ship actually called the Heart."

From somewhere further down the halls, they finally heard Dufresne again. "Is someone there? Houston?"

Before Houston could respond, Bernhard gestured for him to stay quiet. The hall led them directly to another large room, although this one was closer in size to the hangar than the trophy room. In the center of the room was some kind of enormous pillar that glowed with the same unearthly light as the hall, except stronger. All around the pillar there were stairs and catwalks, and where they came in contact with the pillar, there were nodules that brought Bernhard to mind of some kind of computer workstations.

"Is this it?" Johnson whispered. Bernhard understood her sudden need to speak in hushed tones. There was something about the room that brought a certain reverence to him as well.

"Is this what?" Bernhard asked.

"The control room we've been looking for," Johnson said.

"It certainly looks like it could be one," Houston said. "But if it is, I wouldn't have the slightest clue how to operate anything."

"Hello? Bernhard? Johnson? I'm up here!"

Bernhard looked up, trying to find the source of Dufresne's voice. "Dufresne? Where exactly are you?"

"Bernhard? Listen, I'm so sorry I was acting like an asshole to you. Please, you've got to get me out of here."

"All's forgiven, Dufresne," Bernhard said, although that wasn't even close to true. "Just give us some idea of where you are."

"Uh, near the top, I think? The ceiling's only like ten feet above me."

Teng approached Bernhard and spoke quietly into his ear. "There is no way she has not been compromised."

Bernhard nodded. "I agree, but if this is really the room we're looking for, we're going to need to secure it anyway before we start trying to play with any of the Visitor's controls." He spoke up again and directed his voice to the top of the pillar. "Dufresne, I know how hard it is for you, but I'm going to need you to be quiet while we do a sweep of the room."

"Okay," she said with a distinctly resigned and frightened tone. She sounded less like the obnoxious woman he'd been dealing with earlier and more like a scared child. That could simply be because of the experience she'd had, but Bernhard thought it far more likely that she wasn't acting like Dufresne because, simply put, she wasn't Dufresne anymore. She was part of the Nerve, and they were going to have to put her down.

A quick sweep of the lowest area of the room showed them two entrances and three sets of stairs that led up to various parts of the catwalk. Above them, the various catwalks and steps formed a maze upon which any of the Nerve's worms or bodies could be hiding. This was a very bad place to try making a stand, but they had to secure it no matter what.

"Houston, Johnson, and Li," Bernhard said. "You three are going to stay down here and stand in the most open, viewable spot possible, but try not to stand under any of the catwalks where a worm could drop on you from above. Zersky and Chow, you two are going to guard the doors. One of you at each, but maintain line of sight with the scientists at all times, both for their safety and for yours. If you see anything at all moving in the halls beyond, you obliterate it. Teng, take your people and split them into two groups of three. Each group takes one of the stairways going up while I'll go up the third with Hodges and McNeil. Check every possible space you find that could be small enough for a worm to hide, and just like the scientists, watch above you for any place where one could drop on your head. I want this entire room completely and totally secured. Everyone got it?"

They all took their positions, and the three teams of three started up the stairs. They only got up to the first level of catwalks before Dufresne broke her promise to shut up. "Hey, Bernhard? I think the Nerve's setting you up for a trap."

Bernhard didn't answer. He already knew this, of course, and already knew that she would be the point where the trap snapped shut. The only question was what he was going to do to neutralize her. The smartest thing would be to shoot her as soon as they reached her so that she couldn't try that spitting trick on anyone. Houston, however, might have a problem with that, and they needed him to keep working with them. He might be a little hesitant to continue cooperating with them if he happened to witness Bernhard put two bullets in the skull of what used to be his girlfriend.

"Bernhard, can you hear me? The Nerve said something to me about still having bodies hidden in the group. Someone with you is still part of the Nerve but pretending to be human!"

Bernhard motioned for Hodges and McNeil to stop behind them as they were halfway up another set of stairs. He could see Teng's group also stop at Dufresne's words, while Taam's kept going as though they hadn't heard her.

"Captain, it's got to be a trick," McNeil whispered to Bernhard. "The Nerve knows that we're onto it and is trying to make us paranoid against each other again."

"Yeah, besides, you already know that none of us are with the Nerve," Hodges said. "We're all the ones that passed your test, remember?"

Bernhard nodded as though he believed them completely, but his mind was already working. What better way would there have been for one of the Nerve's bodies to gain his trust than to show most of the people it controlled during the fake execution, but still leave one or two hidden within the group? Even if it had just been one left behind, that part of the Nerve could have infected more while everyone's guard had been down again. It was an insidious plan that Bernhard could have easily swallowed hook, line, and sinker.

He tried to push that idea away. McNeil and Hodges were right. This could only be the Nerve trying to mess with them. There was no tactical reason why the Nerve wouldn't have infected Dufresne. She had to be lying.

Then again, he'd been saying exactly that to the group repeatedly ever since the fake execution. If there was indeed still a mole within their group, then the Nerve knew they wouldn't trust Dufresne. It would be a brilliant mind game, then, to *not* infect her, but in fact let them shoot her. In the end, she would be off the board one way or the other and there would be one less human for the Nerve to exterminate while the mole continued to work undetected within the group.

Also, McNeil and Hodges were being *very* insistent that Dufresne still be killed. Possibly too insistent.

Bernhard looked up again to the top of the pillar. He thought he could see Dufresne sitting against the railing of one of the catwalks, possibly with her arms secured behind her back. Her position was actually the perfect position from which someone could attack them. It offered a clear line of sight of all three scientists on the floor, as well as Zersky. As the three military groups ascended, they too could be fired upon. Of course, the Nerve didn't seem to have any weapons, and the weapons its bodies had once wielded were now in the hands of the scientists.

If Dufresne was telling the truth, then the higher they all went and the closer they got to her, the more chance a mole in their group would be able to kill most of them with just a handful of well-placed shots.

Bernhard stopped on the second level of the catwalks.

"Everyone stop!" he called out. He saw the other two groups instantly stop progressing, although they were both at least a level higher than him by now. Both McNeil and Hodges, however, seemed less than pleased with his order.

"Captain, you aren't seriously saying you believe her, do you?" Hodges asked.

"Hodges, McNeil, I want both of you to go back down," Bernhard said.

The two of them stared at Bernhard for a long moment. With each second that ticked by, the silence in the huge room became more and more oppressive.

Then both Hodges and McNeil spit at him.

CHAPTER FOURTEEN

Bernhard was prepared for the attack this time. He easily ducked both worm spitballs, then used slammed the butt of his rifle into Hodges's stomach. He hit with enough force that the man, if he could still be called that anymore, staggered back and hit the railing. Bernhard pressed his advantage and smacked Hodges directly under the chin, causing him to lose what little balance he had left and tumble over the railing. Bernhard didn't have time to look over the side and see whether or not the two-story fall had killed him or not. McNeil had run back down the catwalk just far enough to be out of Bernhard's immediate reach, then turned around, aimed, and fired at him. Bernhard ran right down the catwalk toward the central pillar, putting it between him and McNeil. From below him, he could hear gunfire erupting. Bernhard looked over the edge of the catwalk to see Chow putting a bullet into Hodges as he tried to crawl away, while Zersky concentrated his fire on something Bernhard couldn't see at the far side of the room. The three scientists were shooting – badly – in that direction as well, making Bernhard suspect that was where the two masses of Nerve worms had fallen to the floor and come to a rest. Above him, there were more shouts and sounds of a fight, but from his current vantage point, he couldn't get a clear view of whatever was happening. Someone grunted, someone else screamed, and then Yeow dropped backwards from the catwalk. Apparently, Hodges and McNeil weren't the only ones who were part of the Nerve. Bernhard couldn't take a moment to assess what was going on overhead, though. He had to deal with McNeil.

Bullets hit the pillar as Bernhard hid behind it, although just like in the room earlier, they didn't ricochet. Someone fired at McNeil from above, forcing him to back up onto one of the stairwells and use it for partial cover. That gave Bernhard the chance to peek around the side and line up a shot of his own. It missed, but he could clearly hear McNeil when he spoke. In fact, it wasn't just McNeil speaking, but also Ngai from above as well as the voices of Sorensen, Stroebel, Hatch, and Pai from below, two each coming from beyond both of the doors below. All of the infected members of the team were here, and all of them spoke at once with the words of the Nerve.

"Trying to resist this is foolish," the Nerve said, their voices echoing throughout the entire room. "Even if you stop me here, I still have worms all over the ship. And if I don't destroy you, then the Cortex will as soon as they wake up."

"But the Cortex can't wake up!" Bernhard said. "Aren't the signals from Earth blocking the hive mind from communicating with the soldiers on the Visitor?"

"Houston was right, Bernhard," the Nerve said. "The Visitor does indeed have a Heart. And while I've been working on my duty of exterminating the intruders, the Heart has been fulfilling its own duty. In a short period of time, the Heart will succeed and wake the Cortex. And once that happens, your civilization will join all those others you witnessed in the Trophy Room. All that will remain is to teleport a few of your buildings and weapons in there, and the Visitor will go on to its next world to wipe clean."

Bernhard would have asked the Nerve what the hell it was talking about, but the gunfire started up again. There was a splash of blood from one of the upper catwalks.

"Bernhard!" Teng called down. "We've got Ngai. Let us hold down McNeil, and you find another way down to help Zersky and Chow."

Bernhard called back an affirmative, then took stock of his surroundings. He was too far up to simply jump off the catwalk without serious injury to himself, and McNeil was holding the stairs where he had come up. But from here at the center pillar, he could make his way around the catwalks to some of the stairs that the other two groups had used. Looking over the side again, he saw that, while Stroebel and Hatch were being held back at one door, Pai had managed to get into the room far enough to grab the gun of one of the fallen soldiers. He was laying down enough suppressing fire that Chow, Zersky, and the scientists were starting to back themselves into a corner, which only left more room for Sorensen to get in behind Pai in an attempt to get his own rifle. Bernhard fired a burst in their direction, hitting Sorensen multiple times in the chest. Although he flew back and hit the ground, Sorensen looked like he was still trying to stand back up. Bernhard tried again, this time aiming for Sorensen's head. This time, the body that had up until recently been a United States Army Ranger did not get back up.

Bernhard rushed on down a flight of stairs, then found a position on the catwalks that gave him the opportunity to cover those on the ground. Zersky managed to get a shot off through the door that took out Hatch. For a second, all firing in the room stopped, leaving a moment of silence that the Nerve soon decided to fill up.

"My surprise advantage has diminished, it would seem," the Nerve said through its remaining mouths in Pai, McNeil, and Stroebel. "I suspected that was possible, so I set up a contingency. If you let these three bodies go, I will tell you the location of the thermonuclear bomb that you happened to misplace."

No one spoke as Bernhard considered this proposition. It wouldn't take much more of a fight for them to remove the former Pai, McNeil, and Stroebel from this equation, but knowledge of the bomb's location could be important. However, something didn't seem right about the proposal. It was too easy. He hadn't seen anything yet to disprove the Nerve's claim that it wouldn't lie once exposed, but it had shown that it could still keep secrets. He went over the words the Nerve had just said to them, looking for whatever loophole the alien organism had left for itself. Given that its sole purpose was to destroy them while protecting the Cortex, it didn't make any sense for it to give the bomb back to them. That could only mean that, once it told them where to find the bomb, it would either be in a location that they couldn't reach, or else it had something else planned that would prevent them from getting there. In fact, it seemed likely that the Nerve might even have a backup plan for keeping them from even leaving this room.

"Teng?" Bernhard called up. "Can you hear me?"

"I can."

"How close are you to Dufresne?"

"I have eyes on her now. She's still one story up from our current position."

"Secure her first, then maybe we'll negotiate with the Nerve." Not that he planned to actually do that, but he wanted to buy some time to figure out what the Nerve was up to. Even though the Nerve had had three moles still hiding within their group, this hadn't been the most advantageous of places to make a stand against them. The Nerve would have been better suited waiting until it could infect a few more of them with worms.

Unless, of course, that was exactly what it had planned to do here. Bernhard slowly looked up at the ceiling far overhead. Somewhere in the shadows, he thought he could see something moving.

"They're on the ceiling!" Bernhard yelled. "Everyone take cover!" Just as he finished saying it, worms started to rain down from above.

Bernhard took a position directly underneath one of the catwalks, already realizing the irony of having to do exactly the opposite of he'd warned everyone else against when they'd entered the room. His position didn't allow him to see what might be happening to the groups still above him, but below, he had no choice but to watch as both Chow and Li failed to get out of the way of the worms in time. Chow made a good show of fighting off the worm currently wrapped around his neck, but Li wasn't so lucky. She batted away at the creature, screaming all the while, which only gave the worm a nice open orifice to aim for. With a speed that shouldn't have been possible for something like the worm, it threw itself into her mouth. It appeared to angle itself upward for the back of her soft palette, and for a moment, Bernhard could see the absolute terror and pain as the tiny monster burrowed up into her brain. Then, as the last portion of the worm pulled itself in and disappeared within her, Li's eyes glazed over, soon to be replaced with the same blank look Bernhard had seen on Stroebel's face during the interrogation.

Bernhard only had a moment to line up his shot, but his angle on Li was good. His bullets blew open the back of her head, destroying the worm inside before it had even had a chance to fully assume control. Bernhard could only hope that the poor woman hadn't spent long being aware that everything unique about her was being devoured from the inside out.

Chow managed to wrestle his own worm away, throwing it aside only for a second one to land on him and immediately force itself into his ear. Before Bernhard could try taking him out, Johnson turned around and shot him from only a few feet away. The bullets ripped apart the man's chest and throat before the worm had even completely burrowed itself into Chow's brain, and for one almost comical moment, it looked like the worm was trying to change its mind and back out. Zersky turned on him and fired directly into the ear, finishing the job Johnson had started.

For half a minute, Bernhard became distracted by the worms crawling along the catwalks as he systematically exterminated every single one he could find. Then, when his path appeared to be clear, he finally realized that all shooting had ceased. He looked down again to see that both Pai and Stroebel were dead, along with a large number of worms now shriveling up on the floor. Johnson, Houston, and Zersky stood next to each other, all three of them panting with the exertion.

"Zersky!" Bernhard called down. "Please tell me you're sure that neither Houston or Johnson was infected."

"I'm positive, but how do I know you weren't?" Zersky asked.

"I was keeping an eye on him," Johnson said. "There wasn't any moment where he could have been taken over."

"Teng!" Bernhard said in the direction of the catwalks overhead. "What about you? How do I know none of you were infected?"

"Taam was infected," Teng said with an uncommon note of sadness in his voice. "I had to put him down. I was able to kill McNeil, though, and Dufresne is safe. She and Tshien can both vouch for me, and I can vouch for them."

Bernhard took a deep breath at that. It could be the case that Teng, Dufresne, and Tshien all managed to avoid getting a head full of worms, or it could be that all three of them were now a part of the Nerve and pretending they weren't. However, it seemed unlikely that they would have gotten infected then killed two others that were, so Bernhard decided it was more likely than not that they were safe.

So that meant that all humans infected with the Nerve now appeared to be dead. While that might seem like a cause for celebration, it also meant that their entire team was now reduced to just the three American scientists, two Chinese soldiers, and two Air Force Spec Ops. Considering they still had a whole ship full of sleeping alien warriors to contend with, as well as an unknown number of Nerve worms still waiting to make a play for them at any time, Bernhard considered this particular battle to be a loss. The odds were very much looking to be against them now.

CHAPTER FIFTEEN

There were a few more stray worms they needed to kill, but otherwise, the room with the pillar was secure soon after the battle. Zersky and Tshien guarded the doors while the others gathered up the bodies of the fallen and did their best to lay them respectfully to rest in a far corner. It was highly unlikely that their bodies would ever be retrieved and given a proper send-off back on Earth, but Bernhard wanted them to be somewhere they could find them again if such a thing later became possible. This was followed by an awkward reunion between Houston and Dufresne where they almost but didn't quite kiss. After that, they were all finally free to properly inspect the room they currently found themselves in.

"So is this the control room we were looking for or not?" Bernhard asked.

"Even if it's not, it still must be something important," Houston said. "Those various nodules on the pillar look almost like they could be computer terminals."

Johnson, Houston, Dufresne, Bernhard, and Teng all went up to the first level of catwalks and found the pillar nodules there. Houston stepped forward and examined them more closely. "That clear part there could be a view screen of some sort," Houston said. "But I don't see any kind of input device like a keyboard or anything."

"Then how are we supposed to interact with it?" Dufresne asked.

"Simply ask me and I will help."

The voice seemed to come from everywhere around them. It wasn't even like it came out of hidden loudspeakers somewhere, but rather was caused by a subtle vibration of every single thing in the room. The catwalks, the stairs, the nodules, the pillar, even the walls themselves seemed to be the voice's source. That alone would have been startling enough, but even more so was the fact that the voice sounded like it belonged to a child of maybe six or seven. Bernhard couldn't even determine what gender the voice might be.

"Who said that?" Johnson asked the room.

"I did."

"Yes, but who are you?" Bernhard added.

"The Nerve already told you who I am. I am the Heart."

Bernhard tightened his grip on his rifle. "And are you about to try finishing the job that the Nerve started on us?"

"No. That is not my programming."

Johnson gently touched Bernhard's weapon and made him lower it. When she spoke again, there was a tone in her voice very similar to an adult trying to address a small child that had just wandered up to them, lost and confused. "Heart, what is your programming?"

"It is my function to ensure that the Cortex has all its needs met in order to carry out its mission. This includes control over all forms of life support."

"Why do you sound like a child?" Bernhard asked. "And how is it that you speak English?"

"The Nerve downloaded all the knowledge it had regarding the human species into my memory core, including all languages spoken by those human bodies it took over. I chose this particular voice from all the various signals I am receiving from Earth, as I have determined that it is the one most likely to put you at ease."

"At ease nothing," Dufresne murmured. "This thing sounds creepy as hell."

"Aren't you going to try killing us like the Nerve did?" Bernhard asked.

"There are two problems with that assertion," the Heart said. "The first is that I have no direct means to do so."

"What about indirect means?" Johnson asked.

"There would be plenty of options, but the second issue with your assertion is that I am not programmed to do such. My purpose is to do what I can to sustain life on the ship you refer to as the

Visitor, not take it."

"Good to know we're not going to have all the oxygen suddenly sucked out of the room on us," Bernhard said. "You seem awfully helpful to us so far, considering what we came here to do."

"Again, it is not in my programming to try to impede your progress. You are aboard the Visitor. It is my job to help those aboard the Visitor to maintain life functions. Therefore, it is my job to help you."

"Good to know," Bernhard said. "Except how do we know that anything you're telling us is the truth?"

"It is not in my programming to lie."

"Just like the Nerve," Houston said. "Seems to me like that might be a major oversight by whatever created all of you."

"The intent of our programmers is not important," the Heart said. "Only that the programming be followed."

"It seems like we might have finally caught a break," Bernhard said to the others.

"Maybe," Johnson said. "Although something is bothering me. Hey, Heart?"

"Yes, Dr. Johnson?"

Johnson frowned. "Okay, the mysterious alien computer already knowing my name? That part is a bit creepy. But anyway, the Nerve said something about you while we were fighting it."

"That is correct. It did."

"Specifically, it said that you were working to wake the Cortex up."

"Again, that is correct. The Cortex is not operating optimally at the moment."

Houston made a humorless chuckle. "I suppose that's one way to put it, although it's more like they're not operating at all."

"So you're trying to wake them up," Johnson said to the Heart. "I don't suppose there's any way to convince you not to do that, is there?"

"That would be a violation in my programming in much the

same way that trying to harm you would be a violation."

"But Heart, you *can't* wake the Cortex up," Johnson said. "At least not according to what the Nerve told us. The Cortex's ability to link up with their hive mind is being impeded by Earth's communications."

"That is correct."

Bernhard suddenly got a sinking feeling. "The Visitor has a way to try disrupting all communications from Earth, doesn't it?"

"I am forced to use alternative methods to the problem, but yes. I anticipate that my improvised system will cease all offending communications from Earth when it is ready."

"And how long before it is ready?" Teng asked.

"As time is measured by your species, the improvised system will be capable of disrupting Earth communications in four hours, twenty-eight minutes, and seven seconds."

Everyone went quiet and stared at each other in horror. Even Bernhard, so practiced at schooling his features, was sure that Johnson could easily read on his face what he was thinking. If something stopped the various frequencies from Earth that were blocking the hive mind from communicating with the Cortex, then in under five hours Earth, including Bernhard's own daughter, would be under a vicious, unstoppable alien attack.

"Heart, please! You can't do that!" Johnson begged. "If your function is to maintain life, then surely letting the Cortex attack Earth would be a violation of your programming."

"I am only programmed to aid life through my own actions. Preventing death caused by others is not within my programming. Also, my domain is the Visitor. Events on Earth are not within my purview."

Bernhard nodded. "That's why it didn't do anything at all to intervene on either side while we were fighting the Nerve."

Houston started pacing. "Look, everything about the Visitor and its organic intelligence systems revolves around programming, right? It must fulfill its programming at all costs. But we've already seen that there are loopholes that can be exploited, like how the Nerve stops lying altogether once it's positively revealed. So that's what we've got to do here."

Bernhard nodded thoughtfully. "Heart, what did you mean by an improvised system to shut down Earth communications? What are you doing to make that happen?"

"From the moment the Visitor arrived in orbit around your planet, I have been absorbing radiation into the central systems so that I may rework it and create an electromagnetic pulse that would knock out all electronic devices on Earth. The resulting void in communications noise should be enough for the Cortex to receive its orders from the hive mind."

Teng hissed in a breath. "That will not just break down communications. It will render practically all technology on the planet inoperable."

"Including most of our higher tech weapons," Bernhard said. "Anything more advanced than a gun would be useless. Tanks, fighter jets, nuclear missiles, everything with a computer in it. Earth would be completely defenseless."

"The radiation," Johnson said. "That's why we didn't pick up even the slightest trace of background radiation around the Visitor. It's been siphoning and storing it. But, Heart, have you really been able to gather enough to create an EMP that would affect a whole planet?"

"The process was indeed slow, but I was able to accelerate the plan when another source of radiation was introduced."

Johnson turned to Bernhard. "The nuke. Do you see? That's what happened to it. If you had never allowed it on board, we wouldn't be facing a countdown right now!"

"No, we would still be facing a countdown," Bernhard said, unable to keep a quiver out of his voice. As much as he didn't want to admit it, Johnson was right. "We would just have more time instead of less than five hours. But, Heart, how did you even get the bomb out of the *Ambassador*? And where is it now?"

"Once I determined the source of the additional radiation, I teleported it to a secure vault within the Visitor. There is no way in or out of the vault without teleporting."

"Teleportation," Dufresne said with awe. "Didn't the Nerve mention something about that? Heart, if you can teleport things, can't you just teleport one of us into this vault?"

"For multiple reasons, I cannot."

"What reasons?" Bernhard asked.

"There are three. The first is that teleportation cannot be used on a living organic organism. The process would kill it, thus violating my programming. The second is that, even if the Visitor was equipped with the sort of teleporter that might work on organics, the radiation within the vault would kill whichever of you was sent, thus violating my programming. The third is that allowing any of you to interfere with the process at work in the vault would prevent me from waking up the Cortex, thus violating my programming."

"Programming, programming, programming," Houston muttered to himself. His pacing became more frantic. While this worried Bernhard, both Dufresne and Johnson seemed to take heart in this. Seeing Bernhard's look, Johnson came closer and whispered to him.

"I've seen him do this before. This is how he thinks best. The faster he paces, the closer he is to a solution."

"Well then, by all means, let him keep pacing," Bernhard said. "But in the meantime, the rest of us can't just wait around for a little lightbulb to go off in his head."

"Programming," Houston muttered again. "We have to work within the confines of the programming."

"Maybe there's a way to shut the Heart off and prevent it from doing this," Teng said.

"I would advise against this," the Heart said. "Shutting me down would mean shutting down all life support systems in the Visitor. Doing this would result in your deaths, and assisting you in this regard would be a violation..."

"Of your programming," Bernhard said. "You know what? All the artificial organisms on this ship really like to repeat themselves over and over and over. It's getting kind of annoying."

Houston suddenly stopped pacing and snapped his head to look directly at the pillar. Bernhard supposed that was the closest thing they could do to looking the Heart directly in the eye. "Heart, what *exactly* are you programmed to do regarding the Cortex?"

"I must assist in any way possible in the effort to let the Cortex receive their orders from the hive mind."

"Okay, but what's the process of them receiving those orders?" Houston thought for a second, then added. "Does every Complex soldier in the ship receive their orders at once?"

"They will not. Due to the distances involved between these Cortex soldiers and the center of the hive mind, the order for them to wake and commence the assault on Earth will be staggered. This will also assist in logistics as they are leaving stasis, so they are not all swarming the Visitor at once."

Bernhard exchanged a knowing look with Houston. He thought he understood what Houston might be getting at. "Heart," Bernhard said. "Does your programming specifically say that all the Cortex soldiers on the ship must be awake, or would your programming be considered fulfilled if only a few woke up?"

"My function in waking up the Cortex soldiers is considered fulfilled once the first soldier wakes from stasis."

Now Dufresne seemed to be understanding the idea as well. "So you're saying that if the Visitor was out of the communications haze of Earth for only a moment, allowing only a small group of the Cortex to receive their signal and wake up, you wouldn't have a problem with us doing something to block the signal again after that?"

"That is correct."

Dufresne and Houston looked excited, like they'd come up with the plan to save them all, but Teng looked far from convinced. "But that would not work. Once the Heart sends out the EMP to knock out communications on Earth, the damage to all existing devices would be permanent. The only way to create the communications haze again would be to rebuild every electronic device on Earth from scratch. There would be no way to have the haze back in time to keep every Cortex soldier on this ship from waking up."

Zersky called out from the floor below them. "Yeah, you guys, I've been listening to all of this, and there's another problem. If these Cortex soldiers are as badass as the Nerve said they were, then even waking up a few could still be a problem. If they get down to Earth, we would still have a ton of people die."

Johnson shook her head. "No, don't either of you see? If we managed to wake up a small number of Cortex soldiers *before* the Heart uses the EMP, then it won't have to do that anymore. Right, Heart?"

"That is correct. My programming would then be fulfilled, and I would not be forced to use the electromagnetic pulse."

"Maybe I am missing something," Teng said. "I thought it was not possible to wake any of the Cortex while in the communications haze around Earth."

"It's not," Johnson said. "But, Heart, are you able to move the Visitor? At least if doing such would allow you to fulfill your programming?"

"That is correct."

Johnson looked at everyone else on the catwalk in turn with an impish gleam in her eye. "That's the answer, then. We have the Heart move the Visitor outside of the low Earth orbit it's currently in. The Cortex will receive their signal and wake up once it's outside the range of the communications haze, but the soldiers will also be further from Earth. The few Cortex soldiers that wake up will have a harder time getting to our planet."

"This has all the beginnings of a possibly brilliant plan, Johnson," Bernhard said. "But there's still one key flaw. Once the Visitor is outside the range of the communications haze, then how would we ensure that we only wake up a small number of Cortex soldiers rather than the full army?"

"We would just have the Heart move the Visitor back into the haze," Houston said. "Heart, you could do that, right?"

For the first time, the Heart paused before it spoke as though it were thinking and considering its answer. Finally, it said, "I could not."

Bernhard bristled. "Can't or won't?"

"As much as I would prefer to follow your orders in such a way that would preserve as much life as possible, I could not. The speed with which I would need to move the Visitor in order to get it out of the haze before the pulse went off would create a level of momentum that could not easily be reversed. I would not be able to stop the Visitor and redirect it back into the haze in enough time to keep any of the Cortex in stasis. They would all be awake and aware of their orders before the signal could be blocked again."

The three scientists deflated at that news, but Bernhard was undeterred. "Heart, if you moved us out of the haze, would there be any other way to block the signal from the hive mind?"

"The haze created by human communications is the only thing I have ever been aware of that could block the hive mind's signal."

"How strong do those human communication signals have to be?" Bernhard asked.

"It would not require a lot."

Bernhard smiled. "As in, would the comm equipment we're carrying with us be enough to do the trick?"

"It would not," the Heart said.

Bernhard's smile faltered. So much for that idea.

"What about the equipment on the *Ambassador*?" Johnson asked. "That's powerful to get a signal back to Earth. Wouldn't it be enough to interfere here?"

"It would."

"That's it, then!" Houston said. "We launch someone in the *Ambassador* so it will be out of range of the jamming from inside the ship. Then we move the Visitor, wake up one or two of the Cortex, our badass military guys take them out, and then boom goes the dynamite!"

"Intentionally causing an explosion on the Visitor would run counter to my programming."

"Er, that's not what I meant," Houston said.

While Houston looked ecstatic, Bernhard couldn't help but notice that both Johnson and Dufresne were more subdued. "What's wrong?" he asked. "Do you two see a flaw in the plan?"

"All of this still leaves the Visitor in play," Johnson said. "We have to do more to disable the Visitor and make sure it can't just be put back in range. The EMP will still be like a doomsday weapon just floating above our planet."

"Maybe," Dufresne said, her voice hesitant, "maybe we shouldn't try to bring it back into range of the planet. We could simply have the Heart fly it right out of our solar system."

"But as soon as we leave it with the *Ambassador*, the Cortex would wake up," Teng said.

Bernhard took a deep breath. "You're right. What they're saying is that we're not going to be able to leave."

Houston suddenly lost all his previous joviality. "We would be stuck on the Visitor, forever, as it drifts through space."

Bernhard's heart got heavy. He truly would never see his daughter again, but she would be safe. *Everyone's* daughters and sons would be safe. If the price that needed to be paid for that was that they had to sacrifice their lives, then Bernhard thought he could live with that.

Not for the first time, Bernhard wished he'd been able to bring his MP3 player. If he was going to be stuck floating through the void for the rest of his – probably very short – life, then it would be easier to bear with his beloved Ozzy, with Randy Rhodes' and Zak Wylde's guitar solos, with *Shot in the Dark* and *Crazy Train* and *Bark at the*...

Wait.

"We don't send it just flying off," Bernhard said. "We ground it. Far enough from the Earth that the EMP couldn't be used, yet close enough that we can still get someone to come and get us. And from there, we'll still even be able to harvest it for technology, study it, and all the while maintaining a signal that will keep the rest of the Cortex from waking up."

"Ground it?" Houston asked. "Seriously? The point it to get the Visitor away from it, not land the ship on the planet."

Johnson perked up as she realized what Bernhard was getting at. "The moon?"

Bernhard nodded. "The moon. We ground the Visitor on the moon."

CHAPTER SIXTEEN

By the time they had hammered out all the details of their plan, they were down to four hours before the Heart would set off the EMP. They tried to convince the Heart that the EMP wouldn't be necessary if it just did as they asked it, but the Heart refused, saying that it needed to wake up the Cortex as soon as possible in order to fulfill its programming. Given that, the Heart had agreed to move the Visitor so that it would leave the haze just before it would need to use the EMP. Then, given their current course, it would be another half hour before the Visitor did its rough emergency landing on the moon.

Given the specifics they had worked out, the Heart estimated that roughly two hundred and fifty Cortex soldiers would receive their order from the hive mind before they were able to block the signal again. So the next four hours had to be dedicated to making sure, once they were awake, it wouldn't seem like such an unfair fight when a couple hundred aliens intent on planetary destruction took on four soldiers and three scientists.

The bad news for this portion of the plan was that, no matter where they went and what they did to prepare, the team couldn't split up. There were still Nerve worms out there, and the Heart had insisted that it was not within its programming to interfere with the Nerve's machinations. The Heart wouldn't even tell them where the Nerve might be hiding. The good news, however, was that the Heart was being helpful in all other things, provided they didn't interfere with their programming. This included doing a certain amount of rearranging of things at Bernhard's request. While he had doubted that the Heart would be able to do it so quickly, everything was prepared for them when they finally made it back to the hangar. All but three of the boxes containing the Cortex fighter ships were gone. The Heart had agreed to transport them elsewhere within the Visitor, under the condition that it wasn't expected to damage any of them. In place of that large, startling fleet were three new vehicles: two of the mechs and one of the crab tanks they had seen in the trophy room. This was what they were going to use to fight off the Cortex soldiers.

The Heart, thankfully, assured them that it could transfer a portion of itself into each of the seven vessels, including the *Ambassador*, for as long as the vehicles remained in physical contact with the Visitor. Once they took off or left, each one would be flying solo.

"I still don't know if putting me in one of these things is a good idea," Houston said as they entered the hangar and took in its now relative emptiness. "You all saw how bad a shot I was with a normal human rifle, so how the hell am I going to be able to operate some kind of alien war vehicle?"

"I will be able to teach each of you the most basic controls in the vehicles you inhabit," the Heart said. The voice had followed them the whole way back, speaking by vibrating the halls around them. Bernhard had almost gotten used to the disembodied voice when he'd been able to think of it as residing within the pillar. But now that it was out and following them around the ship, there was no way not to think of it as creepy again.

"Everyone pick a vehicle," Bernhard said. "We've got roughly three and a half hours to learn how to use them."

"I call one of the fighter ships!" Zersky said with a near child-like glee. Bernhard almost hated to disappoint him. Almost.

"No can do, Zersky. You're going to need to man the *Ambassador*. It's going to be tough enough with just one person flying it, but I also need someone who'll be able to keep up alongside the Visitor as it rushed along to its final destination. Remember, if the *Ambassador* and the Visitor get too far apart, more Cortex soldiers will wake up, and we're already up against pretty impossible odds as it is."

Zersky did his best to hide his disappointment. Bernhard couldn't help but smile.

"Relax. I'm sure there will be plenty of opportunities in the future for you to fly an alien fighter craft in battle."

As the group broke up and went in their prospective directions, all of them staying within sight of each other up until the last possible moment to prevent possession by the Nerve, Johnson stayed behind long enough to say a few words to Bernhard.

"Can you really believe that those words just came out of your mouth?" Johnson asked. The seven of them were the only people standing between an army of alien invaders and billions of unsuspecting people on Earth, yet somehow she looked for a moment like she might actually be having fun. And as much as it behooved Bernhard to admit it, he definitely saw the appeal. Johnson wasn't the only one who watched a large number of sci-fi movies, after all. Bernhard might have been able to fly highly experimental aircraft in the past that most people couldn't dream of, but he had already called one of the mechs for himself on the way here. No matter how well-trained the military had made him at hiding his emotions, even he couldn't deny that there was a part of him that kind of thought this was awesome.

He didn't let those thoughts stay in him for long, though, and he needed to make sure they didn't stay with Johnson, either. "Jane, we're about to face down an army of advanced aliens, and over half our team is dead. We need to stay focused and realize there's not a very good chance of us surviving this."

Johnson looked taken aback. "That's the first time you've called me Jane instead of Johnson."

"Out of everything I've just said, that's all you took away from it?"

"Look, Bernhard, uh, Captain, er…actually, I don't think I even know your first name?"

"Not that it matters, but it's James."

"James, I'm very much aware of what the stakes are and how unlikely it is that we'll be walking away from it. Which is why I thought it was important to say, uh…"

Bernhard cocked his head. "Johnson, don't. Even if we do survive this, there's no chance of us ever being together. Our lives are too different, and neither of us would be willing to make a change for the other. So if you're expecting this to be the part where we share some dramatic kiss, then I'm sorry to embarrass you. But we can't and shouldn't."

"Huh? Um, Bernhard, I was just going to say that I think your daughter would be proud of you. And, uh, that's all I was going to say."

It took every ounce of Bernhard's will to keep himself from blushing. "Oh. Uh, yes."

"You really thought I wanted to kiss you?" Johnson asked.

"No! Of course not. It's just, um…"

"Bernhard, I think you'll make an excellent father to your daughter when you're finally ready to go to her, but as far as me? You're not my type."

"Of course not."

They stared at each other in awkward quiet for several moments before both of them, through mutual silent agreement, turned around and headed to their respective vehicles for their crash course in alien piloting.

This? This right here? Bernhard thought. *This is why I'll always be career military. Fighting off alien invaders? Easy. Trying not to look like an ass in front of the opposite sex? I'll never get it.*

CHAPTER SEVENTEEN

"…and that is how you should operate inertial dampeners as designed for Kroptoid physiology," the Heart said.

"Heart, has anyone ever told you that you're a terrible teacher?" Bernhard asked.

"No, they have not," the Heart said. "This is the first time I have attempted to teach anyone anything."

And it shows, Bernhard thought to himself, but he prided himself on picking things up quickly, so he was confident that he would be able to operate the mech with minimal embarrassment to himself. He was experienced in getting behind the controls of new, previously untested vehicles, however. If he was having trouble learning the ins and outs of Kroptoid mechs, then he suspected some of the other remaining members of the team were doing worse.

"You said 'Kroptoid,'" Bernhard said. "I'm assuming that would be the name of the alien race this once belonged to?"

"The Kroptoids were the race indigenous to a planet they called…" The Heart made a noise somewhere between a hiss and a hiccough. "They were the first race eliminated by this offshoot of the Cortex."

"And you had no problem with that?" Bernhard asked.

"I am not programmed to have any concern for beings outside the Visitor."

"Yet you're helping us now. Why?"

"You are aboard the Visitor."

"But all the people we're trying to save aren't. And I could already list a half dozen things you've done to help us that can't really be considered central to your programming of maintaining the ship's life support. So again, why?"

For a long time, there was no answer. Bernhard began to

suspect that something had gone wrong and the Heart was no longer functioning.

"Heart? Are you still there?"

"In the last three hours, you are the fourth member of your group to ask me that question."

"And how did you answer the other three?"

"I did not have an answer, and I still do not."

"Maybe that's just the inevitable byproduct of you being programmed to generally protect life. Eventually, you actually start caring about it."

"That is the same thing that Dr. Jane Johnson said to me. Perhaps it is an idea that requires further thought."

At the mention of Johnson, he felt himself blush again. It would be no use going back to those thoughts, not when they were so close to the end of this and he needed to keep his concentration. "Heart, are you able to take what I'm saying and broadcast it to all the others the same way you're doing to us?"

"I can. Go ahead and speak, but do remember that this connection can only go between vessels that are physically touching the Visitor in some manner."

"Alright everyone, this is Bernhard. I hope you've enjoyed your crash courses as well as I have, because we only have twenty minutes to go before the Visitor exits the haze. Here's the battle plan based on everything the Heart has told me. Zersky, I trust the *Ambassador* is ready to go?"

"About as ready as it can be, Captain. It's like I said earlier: these old shuttles aren't designed for these kinds of take-offs, but with the Heart's help, I think I've got everything ready."

"The *Ambassador* is to launch five minutes before the Visitor leaves the haze. Zersky, while you'll be able to contact Earth once you're out of the Visitor, we won't be able to talk to you. So according to the Heart, you will need to keep the comms down for exactly one minute and twenty-two seconds after the Visitor leaves the haze. That's how long it will take for enough of the Cortex to wake up to fulfill the Heart's programming. If you turn it on too early, the Heart will be forced to go back into the haze and set off the EMP. Too late, and the two hundred and fifty alien soldiers we'll be fighting will become a whole lot more. The *Ambassador* must stay within range of the Visitor at all times. When the Visitor grounds on the moon, the *Ambassador* has to go with it. It cannot come back in at any point or the jamming will take out its signal again. Hopefully, at that point, the rest of us will still be alive, and you can use one of the space suits to get back to us after you've told command back on Earth what happened and that we'll need an extraction. Any questions, Zersky?"

"None at all. I'm ready to do this."

The rest of the plans consisted mostly of positioning the six alien vehicles in the most optimal way to fight off the Cortex. According to the Heart, they would wake unaware that anything had gone wrong and that they had been stuck in stasis for an extra week and a half. They would be armed, but they wouldn't be expecting an attack from within the ship itself. Since the hive mind would not be able to communicate with them to change their orders when they got into the hangar and found all their fighter craft missing, their tactical abilities would theoretically be minimal. Bernhard wasn't planning on counting on that, though. Whoever had "programmed" all the life forms they'd encountered on the Visitor so far, they hadn't done very well at filling in gaps in the programming. That would likely make the Cortex more unpredictable than they should be. Bernhard wanted them all to be prepared for anything.

"T-minus five minutes and counting," Zersky said. "This is the *Ambassador* signing off. Good luck to everyone." The old shuttle trundled out of the hangar, and the instant the wheels left the floor and it was out the Visitor's door, they lost all contact with Zersky. He was a good pilot, so Bernhard wasn't too worried, but so much depended on him being able to fly a machine that had existed since before he was born. A hundred things could go wrong, and all it would take was one to cause a chain reaction that would lead to the end of humanity.

"Everyone else, get into position," Bernhard said. "Sound off. Teng?"

"I am go."

"Tshien?"

"Ready."

"Dufresne?"

"Wait, am I supposed to say 'ready' or 'I'm go?' I'm confused."

"Dufresne, seriously."

"Um, ready, I guess."

"Houston?"

"Oh my God, I think I'm going to be sick."

"Uh, does that mean…?"

"I'm go."

"Johnson?"

"My body is ready."

"Er, okay. And this is Bernhard, ready. Does anybody have any last words?"

"Last words? Why would you say that? Seriously, I think…"

"Not you, Dufresne. I mean anybody else?"

No one responded. According to the countdown the Heart had been keeping inside his mech, they had less than two minutes before the Visitor crossed out of the haze. Two minutes before combat. Two minutes until they found out if their meager little force would be enough to keep all of humanity safe. He'd been in combat before, and he wanted to think that this was no different than any other mission he had been in as part of the 843rd Special Operations Squadron. Except there was no comparing the scale. This was the biggest, most important thing he had ever done in his life.

And I'm doing it for you, baby girl, he thought. *If I don't make it out of this, I hope you have a long and happy life.*

The countdown hit zero. A part of him had almost expected the entire Visitor to rumble with the momentous occasion, but mostly he knew better. They were simply passing outside an invisible line, and right now, in that very first room they had entered upon going deeper into the Visitor, hundreds of stasis tubes were opening to let out their deadly, single-minded occupants. The three fighter crafts, piloted by Teng, Houston, and Dufresne, lifted off from their spots on the hangar floor to hover at key areas around the hangar that provided them the best sniping points. On the ground, Bernhard took the middle spot between Tshien in the other mech and Johnson in the crab tank. If things went exactly according to plan, the Cortex soldiers would march right into the ambush and be cut down before more than just a handful could return fire.

Bernhard had plenty of experience that said things never went according to plan.

At first, he thought the vibrating of his mech was coming from the Heart again, but it didn't speak. Apparently, it had gone back into its mode of conscientious objector, although whatever communications mojo it had worked on them still allowed him to speak with Tshien and Johnson. Instead, the vibration was coming through the floor. Judging from the rhythmic way he could feel it in his bones, the Cortex soldiers were all marching in perfect step with each other.

Except, he realized, given the advanced technology of the Visitor, he doubted that a mere two hundred and fifty soldiers would be enough to make the floor shake.

"Bernhard, I think something's wrong," Johnson said.

"I think you're right," Bernhard responded. Something had to have gone wrong with Zersky. Either the comm equipment on the *Ambassador* was not strong enough to block the hive mind's signal after all, or else the rickety old shuttle wasn't keeping proper pace with the Visitor. Whatever the case, they had no way of knowing for sure. As long as he was out there and they were in here, they couldn't get any idea of what might be wrong.

Not only were they about to fight a much larger number of the Cortex than they had originally planned, but if the Cortex was able to communicate with the hive mind during the actual fight, they wouldn't just blunder right into their ambush. The Cortex would be coordinated, hundreds and hundreds of elite alien shock troops versus six people in advanced weaponry they barely understood.

I'm never going to see my daughter again, Bernhard thought. Rather than dampen his spirits, that thought steeled him for the battle to come. *At the very least, I can make her mother tell her heroic stories about me.*

Bernhard put his hands on the controls, preparing to use the mech's laser cannon to cut a swath through the Cortex the instant he saw the first one through the door. Their position would create a bottleneck for the soldiers, and hopefully their unexpected numbers would work against them as bodies fell and blocked the path of those still marching.

Bernhard tightened his fingers on the unusually shaped triggers. "Okay, everyone. Here we –"

Right as he saw the first hint of a Cortex soldier coming at them from down the hall, something smashed into his mech from the side and sent it sprawling on the hangar floor. Bernhard smashed his head against a protruding piece inside the cockpit, and for too many precious seconds, all he could see was a brilliant blue-white flash across his vision.

As his sight came back to him fully, he realized the mech was lying flat on its back. Through the cockpit window, Bernhard saw Tshien in his own mech staring at him. The mech's bladed melee weapon was out, and from the look of the mech's stance, that was what it had used to knock Bernhard's down. Inside Tshien's cockpit, Tshien stared back at him with a blank stare that Bernhard had come to recognize quite well by now.

"Hello again," the Nerve said, speaking through Tshien's vocal cords. "I cannot allow any of you to continue in this course of action."

CHAPTER EIGHTEEN

Multiple thoughts went through Bernhard's head all at once. The first was that the Nerve had to have positioned worms in Tshien's mech. It was the only way he could think of that Tshien might have been compromised. The second was that, if it could have happened to Tshien, then any number of the others could have also been taken over by now. The third thought was that Zersky could have been one of them. If he had been, then this was all over. The Nerve, working through the body of Zersky, had to do nothing more than wait this all out as the *Ambassador* floated aimlessly through space. With no one turn on the shuttle's comm equipment to block the hive mind's signal, the Cortex would continue waking up and continue coming at them like hardened tactical units rather than mindless marching drones.

I can't allow myself to believe that, even for a second, Bernhard thought. Not that he even had time to dwell on that, as Tshien's mech was rearing back with its blade like it was preparing to ram it straight through the cockpit and into Bernhard's prone body. Before it could, however, Johnson's crab tank ran straight into it with enough force that Tshien's mech flew a good fifty feet through the air before it hit the floor and skidded to a halt face down. The six mechanical legs on the tank pivoted it so Bernhard could see Johnson through her own canopy. With one of the tank's four manipulator arms, she grabbed Bernhard's mech and helped right him.

"He's down, but he won't stay that way," Johnson said. "One of us has to take him out."

"You concentrate all your fire on the Cortex," Bernhard said. "I'll go for the Nerve."

"But how are you going to –?"

"For once just do what I say without questioning orders,

Johnson!"

She turned the tank back around to face the oncoming horde. Although the fighter ships had taken out a number of soldiers already, it was obvious that just through sheer numbers the Cortex could overwhelm them quickly, and that was before any of them had even brought their weapons to bear. Johnson activated a beam on her tank that wiped out the entire front row of Cortex soldiers, but the beam apparently needed time to recharge. In the meantime, the next emotionless soldiers in line marched over the charred bodies of their fallen comrades. Bernhard had hope that these vehicles, advanced as far as humans were concerned, would be enough, but that was when they had believed they were facing a much smaller number. Now, with the Cortex continuing to wake up and march mercilessly for them, Bernhard couldn't help but remember that the three ground vehicles were, in fact, the weapons of the losers.

And one of those vehicles wasn't even fighting at their side. As much as Bernhard wished he could turn around and face the Cortex right beside Johnson, he couldn't do that as long as they were fighting this battle on two fronts. If nothing else, Bernhard's duty now was to keep the Nerve occupied while the others continued their defense.

Moving as fast as his inexperienced hands could make the mech go, Bernhard ran over to where Tshien's mech was struggling to get back up. Using his own melee blade, he slashed down at the mech's knee, or whatever the equivalent was called in something where the joint bent backwards. He'd hoped the attack would be enough to sever part of the leg, but whatever the Kroptoids had used to build these things was apparently too strong to give under just one blow.

Before Bernhard could try striking again, Tshien's mech executed a complicated twist and flip, bringing it back to its feet and in a fighting stance.

"Bernhard, you will not win this fight," the Nerve said. "I have not only the knowledge I took from your teammates, but also the Kroptoids that I killed long ago. I know how to operate this machine in a way you never could."

Bernhard was about to make some kind of snarky rejoinder before pressing the attack again, then thought better of it when it occurred to him that this was his chance for a little extra intel. "Do you really need to try killing us now?" Bernhard asked. "You've already got Zersky. As long as you control him, the rest of us will be helpless."

"I do not know what you are talking about. I have not yet taken over Zersky's body."

Bingo, Bernhard thought. Tshien, being now revealed as part of the Nerve, couldn't lie. And that meant that Zersky was still out there, struggling to do his duty, and there was still a chance for them in here.

Bernhard almost sat and contemplated this for too long. Tshien rushed at him with the mech's blade, only barely missing Bernhard as he dodged. While Bernhard's pride wanted to make him think that he really could take out the Nerve in a mech, he knew better. The Nerve was right that it would be able to do things with the mech Bernhard could only dream of, so the longer the two of them fought, the lower Bernhard's chances were of survival.

Bernhard had to do something to make this fight end quickly, long before the Nerve could wear him down. Bernhard looked around for anything he might be able to use to help, but the hangar was now empty except for the two mechs, the crab tank, and the fighters flying overhead as they tried to vaporize the ever-approaching lines of the Cortex. There was nothing else to the hangar but the hangar itself.

And, Bernhard suddenly realized, the massive gaping door that led directly into space. There might have been some kind of field over it preventing explosive decompression, but the *Ambassador* had both come and gone through it with no problem. And if the shuttle could go through it, so, he assumed, could a mech.

Bernhard let Tshien keep attacking, doing his best to act like he had so little control over the mech that all he could do was back up and try not to get hit. With each attack and step back, the two mechs got closer to the hangar door and the gaping void waiting beyond. Once Bernhard thought they were close enough, he finally started to attack again, this time moving so that, instead of having him back to the door, the two of them fought parallel to it. As Tshien made another rush at him, Bernhard did the same, the two of them coming together in the middle with their blades crossed and ringing throughout the hangar. The two mechs strained against each other, both of them trying to gain just enough leverage to topple over the other.

"I know what you are trying to do, Bernhard," the Nerve said. "You think you can find a way to shove me out into space. That does not look like that is working very well for you."

And Bernhard had to admit that it wasn't. The Nerve's control over its mech was simply more fine-tuned than Bernhard. His mech's feet scraped across the floor, inching closer and closer to the edge. Unless he did something drastic, the Nerve was about to send Bernhard's mech out the door instead.

Bernhard had a flash of an idea. His mech was about to float away into the cold emptiness of space, but that didn't mean he had to still be in it when it did.

"Heart, if you can hear me, turn off my communication with Tshien's suit."

"It is now turned off."

"I'm going to need another mech very quickly here. Can you teleport another one into the hangar? Away from where anyone is fighting?"

He didn't have the time to wait for the Heart's answer. Tshien's mech made one last violent shove, and Bernhard let it happen. Instead of simply accepting his fate, however, Bernhard locked one of the mech's arms around Tshien's blade and pulled hard right as Tshien pushed. Before he could think about how idiotic this was, Bernhard opened up his cockpit and ejected out, flying over the Nerve and its commandeered mech. He looked back over his shoulder just long enough to see the two mechs, both of them entangled together, fall out the door and then drift into space. Inside the cockpit, Bernhard could see the Nerve flailing about, desperately trying to figure out some way to get the mech back inside, but soon afterward, the body of Tshien spasmed and ceased moving. Bernhard's earlier concern about Zersky had been unwarranted, he realized. Outside of the jamming signal preventing all human communications inside the Visitor, the Nerve was apparently subject to the same haze that had blocked the Cortex.

Bernhard hit the ground right as a new mech materialized nearby. If the Nerve could no longer speak to the worms inhabiting Tshien's body, yet the Visitor was outside the haze directly around Earth, then that could only mean that Zersky had pulled through on his part of the mission. All Bernhard needed to do now was get back in his mech and help mop up the remaining Cortex.

Not that the battle looked like it was going in their favor once he was strapped back in a mech and heading back to join the others. The Cortex were still coming at them like little more than zombie drones, but enough had pulled their weapons to cause some damage. One of the fighters – Houston's, from the looks of it – was wobbling badly and belching dark smoke from a ruined engine. Johnson's crab tank was immobilized, as it was so deep in dead Cortex bodies that they covered the first joint on its robotic legs.

"Heart!" Bernhard called out as he joined in firing on the advancing aliens. "Are you able to tell us how many Cortex soldiers awoke?"

"One thousand and seventy-five."

"And how many are still coming down the hall towards us?"

"Seventy-three."

"Wait, really?" He suddenly realized that the waves coming at them were indeed thinning out, and he could actually count down the number of remaining Cortex soldiers as they came through the door only to be mowed down by laser weapons. They were almost there. Against impossible odds, it would seem that they'd actually succeeded.

"Correction," the Heart said. "An additional three hundred soldiers have just woken up."

"How is that possible?" Bernhard asked, but he knew the answer as the entire ship around them started to violently rumble and shake. The floor shook so hard that Bernhard's mech lost its balance, and one of the fighters hit a vibrating wall, causing it to careen out of control.

That would be the Visitor grounding on the moon, Bernhard realized. And in the process, the delicate balance that was the distance between the Visitor and the *Ambassador* had been disrupted. It seemed they had no choice but to fight one final battle for the fate of all of humanity.

CHAPTER NINETEEN

"Bernhard, there is one additional complication you might wish to know about."

Bernhard could hear the Heart's voice, but he couldn't see anything at the moment. This time, his mech had fallen face-first into a smoking pile of Cortex bodies, and all he could see was their charred, alien features grinning at him with dead rictuses. He'd had his bell rung again in the fall, so it took him a few seconds to recognize the novelty of the Heart offering up unsolicited information.

"What is it?" Bernhard asked. He fiddled with the controls of his mech, found that most of them still appeared to be functional, and then began the laborious process of putting the mech back in an upright position. "And why are you even trying to tell me?"

"I have come to a decision. I do not want so many human lives destroyed. I would also rather you not kill any more of the Cortex, but I understand there is a matter of scale to consider."

"So what's the complication?"

"The Visitor is back within the range of the *Ambassador*'s comm devices, as the *Ambassador* has grounded only a short distance away from the hangar entrance. But before it set down on your moon, one last change of directive was sent from the hive mind to the woken Cortex soldiers."

"Do I even want to ask?"

"I cannot judge whether or not you want to, but I do suggest you should."

"Don't be so literal. What did the hive mind tell the Cortex to do?"

"The Cortex soldiers are now aware that the *Ambassador* is the only thing keeping them from receiving further instructions from the hive mind. They have been instructed to destroy it so that the remaining tens of thousands of Cortex soldiers may wake from stasis."

"Well, unless they can breathe completely without atmosphere, I guess it's a good thing that there's a bit of distance between the Visitor and the *Ambassador*."

As the mech was once again in its proper position, Bernhard turned it around to properly see the damage the Visitor's crash had done to the hangar.

The hangar was once more full of alien fighter craft. This time, there were no boxes storing them. All of the fighters were now out in the open and waiting for their alien pilots.

"Heart, what the hell did you do?" Bernhard asked.

"I was ordered by the Cortex to put all fighter craft back in their place. I am sorry. It is against my programming to disobey certain orders, no matter what the cost."

"Then how much time do we have until the next batch of the Cortex make it to the hangar and start trying their attack against the *Ambassador*?"

"This group was let out from a farther stasis room, so they will not arrive for roughly five minutes."

"Please tell me that someone else has been listening in on this?" Bernhard asked.

"I heard it," Johnson said.

"So did I," Dufresne said. Bernhard saw that her fighter had been the one knocked about by the crash. It was now broken and lying against a far wall. As he watched, the woman climbed out of her busted craft and ran with a distinct limp to another fighter. She was bleeding from multiple wounds, and yet she didn't let that stop her. Maybe Bernhard was going to need to reassess his attitudes regarding her.

The sight of Dufresne's crashed fighter gave him an idea. "Everyone, before the next wave gets here, destroy as many of the fighters as you can."

"On it," Johnson said. The crash had shaken her crab tank out of the worst of the pile of bodies, allowing her to extricate it the rest of the way out now. Before Bernhard could even give her any advice on how she might destroy them, Johnson's tank walked right over the first fighter craft in line, spearing it with the tank's legs and manipulator arms. Obviously, she didn't need his help.

Floating overhead, Teng's ship appeared to be completely undamaged, and upon seeing what Johnson was doing, he immediately followed suit, concentrating first on the fighters closest to the hall door. Houston's craft hovered for a moment, looking for all the world like it was about to fall out of the air all by itself, before it flew over to a far side of the hangar to land. Houston got out and ran for a new fighter just as Dufresne took off in her new one and followed the example of her teammates.

"Heart, make sure Houston is filled in on everything before his ship takes off again," Bernhard said. He started to blast the fighters one by one, although they proved a bit more resilient to the mech's weapons than they did the others. "Also, keep giving me a countdown until the Cortex gets here."

"The first Cortex soldiers will be in the hangar in the next thirty seconds."

"Wait, what? You just said –"

"This group is no longer marching at the same pace as the others. Not only are they attempting to do their job faster, but..."

Bernhard nodded. "But they're not going to just blunder blindly into our weapons like last time." He ceased his attempts at destroying the fighters and again turned back to the hall door. "Heart, can you give me a running tally of how many Cortex soldiers are left?"

"I would rather not. I do not like continually announcing deaths."

"It would make it much easier to prevent a whole lot more deaths later, Heart."

The Heart paused, but not before making a noise that sounded suspiciously like a sigh. "Three hundred. And the first will be coming in momentarily."

Bernhard was firing the mech's energy cannon before the first Cortex soldiers had even made it into his line of sight.

Surprisingly, though, the Heart didn't announce the number going down at all. These soldiers appeared to be armed differently than the previous ones, including energy shields that they were able to erect in front of themselves before they returned fire. Bernhard had to maneuver his mech out of the way as twenty blasts of laser fire converged on his previous position.

"Johnson, I think I'm going to need help on this one!" Bernhard called out. Before she could turn her crab tank around and go for the new arrivals, however, several shots hit the tank's legs and incapacitated it.

"Johnson, are you okay?" Bernhard asked.

"Just peachy," she said. "I still have weapon systems on this thing, but none of them are terribly long range. If I want to continue contributing anything important to this fight, I'm going to need to switch to one of the fighters. Cover me!"

Bernhard called out for her to stay put, but she was already coming out of the hatch in the top of the tank. Bernhard did his best to lay down cover fire, and he even heard the Heart drop the total number of Cortex soldiers by seven, but all his concentration remained on Johnson as she dodged laser blasts and made a beeline for the nearest fighter she hadn't wrecked. Just like Dufresne, she showed a level of courage and determination in her run that Bernhard would not have expected. He would make proper soldiers out of them yet.

The three fighters that were already in the air turned their attention away from destroying ships and back at holding back the Complex, but Bernhard could see that a small number of troops had already gotten past the door and were huddling in the hangar, waiting for the best opportunity grab a fighter for themselves and head out on their mission.

"There are currently two hundred and twenty-one Cortex soldiers remaining," the Heart said. Another group of them split off from the others and tried to take a different path to the fighters. Bernhard took most of them out, but multiple other groups started taking the same tactic. Too many were getting through the door and into the hangar now. While the number continued to drop, Bernhard realized the various Cortex groups were preventing too many targets. They needed to fall back and regroup at the hangar door, where they could hopefully create another choke point for any Cortex fighters trying to leave the Visitor, but with everyone else now in fighters rather than ground vehicles, he had no way of conveying his commands. He would simply have to go that direction himself and hope that the others followed suit.

"One hundred and sixty-three Cortex soldiers remaining."

Bernhard backed all the way up to the hangar door, but didn't yet step out. The way the Visitor had landed, there would be something of a drop from the door to the surface of the moon. Once he left, the mech would not easily be able to get back in, nor would he be able to communicate with the Heart anymore. Teng's fighter wheeled about in the air and flew to take a position over Bernhard, while one of the others joined him. The remaining two – Dufresne and Houston, he believed – continued to fly around taking potshots at the Cortex. Soldiers had stopped filing through the hall door by now, and a number of them had made it to ships. One of the fighters started to rise in the air, but one of the scientists shot it before it got a few feet off the ground. It crashed into several other fighters, taking a few Cortex soldiers with it.

"One hundred and nine Cortex soldiers remaining."

Several more of the fighters lifted off. All of them at once concentrated their fire on one of the scientists' ships, causing the thing to go out of control. Bernhard had no idea whether it was Houston or Dufresne, but whoever was piloting it aimed the falling and flaming ship at the largest concentration of soldiers still on the ground. Both the fighter and soldiers exploded in a small fireball.

Despite himself, Bernhard really hoped that hadn't been Johnson.

"Fifty-nine Cortex soldiers remaining."

The Cortex soldiers that were now in the fighters were starting to come this way. As any that got past would have free reign to go after the *Ambassador*, Bernhard decided it was finally time for the last fall back. He took a few last shots from his current position, then turned the mech and jumped out of the Visitor to the moon's surface below. His fall was slow, given the barely existent gravity here, and it gave him time to twist the mech around and aim at the door. Three ships backed out after him slowly, firing back in the whole time. The instant a fighter tried to come through that was facing the other way, however, Bernhard unloaded on it. Once he hit the ground, it took him a moment to adjust before he once again started running in the direction of the shuttle.

The *Ambassador* looked like it had suffered a rough landing, but as Bernhard got closer, he could just barely see the hint of a figure through the tinted front windows. Bernhard took a position in front of the shuttle and again turned around. This would have to be the point of the last stand. The old rust-bucket of a space shuttle wasn't designed for combat, and it had already taken far more of a beating than it had ever been designed for. All it would take was a single Cortex fighter getting past him to get a good shot off and destroy their last chance at protecting the Earth.

The firefight at the door flared up as the three remaining ships on his side continued to back away and spread out, giving them a better position to snipe anything that tried to make it through. A single rogue shot from one of the Cortex hit one of the ships, but unlike the previous one, this one managed to crash a little more gently on the moon's surface.

And through it all, a single ship made it out the door and headed directly for Bernhard and the *Ambassador*.

It could have gone high, taking up a position that Bernhard would not have easily been able to defend against from the ground, but instead it went low, skimming the gray surface of the moon and kicking up a trail of dust behind it that hung in the air for a preternatural amount of time. It fired directly at Bernhard, and despite his best efforts to dodge, one of the shots hit the mech in the laser cannon.

The cannon went dead. Now the only thing standing between this single Cortex ship and the end of the human race was a mech armed only with a blade on one arm.

Bernhard breathed deeply, then jammed forward on the controls. The mech leaped in the air just as the Cortex ship tried to pull up and go over him.

Instead, the ship ran right into the blade.

The impact was enough to knock Bernhard's head against the inside of the cockpit, and his world went black. The last thing he saw was the Cortex fighter spinning uncontrollably off into space, completely missing the *Ambassador*.

CHAPTER TWENTY

Bernhard woke up in the familiar confines of the *Ambassador* with Johnson staring down at him, her face full of concern.

"Oh thank God, it's about time," she said. Bernhard tried to sit up from where he had been lying down, but the effort made his aching head pulse with renewed pain.

"How long was I out?" Bernhard muttered.

"You've been here with me in the *Ambassador* for about half an hour," Johnson said. "But you were out cold inside the mech for longer than that. We were starting to get worried that you'd had too little oxygen in there and suffered some kind of brain damage."

"Who's we?" Bernhard asked. In response, Zersky came into view.

"Welcome back, Captain," he said.

"We're not dead," Bernhard said. Johnson smiled.

"No, we're not."

"And Earth?"

"Also not dead," Zersky said. "I've been in contact with command on and off for the last twenty minutes. They know everything that happened, or at least an abbreviated version of it."

"I don't suppose it's too much to hope that all of this is still a secret?" Bernhard asked.

"Oh yeah, definitely too much," Johnson said. "Apparently, anyone with a high-enough-powered telescope could see the battle all the way from Earth. All those attempts you made at clandestine secrecy didn't last long."

Bernhard supposed that was for the best. There would still be an arms and technological race between countries to capitalize on all the tech they might be able to pull off the Visitor, but if all the countries of the world had witnessed that there was a much deadlier threat out here than each other, maybe they would be able to look beyond their own personal paranoias and work together to be prepared in the future.

"Where's Teng and uh...?" Bernhard trailed off, realizing he wasn't sure yet who had been killed.

"Dufresne," Johnson said quietly. "Houston was the one in the ship that took out so many of the Cortex soldiers. He died a hero."

"Yes," Bernhard agreed. "He did."

"Both Teng and Dufresne are back in the Visitor. Don't worry, Teng is being very careful about making sure that neither of them are in a position to be taken over by the Nerve, although we haven't seen any sign of the Nerve since the battle."

"Why not just have them come back to the *Ambassador*?" Bernhard asked.

"Not enough air here," Zersky said. "We're going to have to go back to the Visitor soon as well if we don't want to suffocate. Teng already ordered that one of us come out here every so often to make sure that the comm equipment keeps working, but otherwise, the Visitor is going to be our home for at least the next two weeks."

"Two weeks?" Bernhard asked. "Why?"

"Your brain must still be a little scrambled if you can't yet figure it all out for yourself," Zersky said.

"Bernhard, they already had a hard enough time organizing our mission to the Visitor on such a short notice. Mounting a full rescue operation for us, as well as sending additional scientists and military personnel to keep the Visitor secure, isn't going to be a quick job."

Bernhard nodded, a motion that he instantly regretted as the headache flared again.

"We'll be taking one of the Cortex ships back to the Visitor as soon as Dr. Johnson says you're ready to travel," Zersky said.

"In the meantime, could you give us a couple of minutes by ourselves?" Johnson asked Zersky. Zersky gave her a knowing smile.

"Sure. I'll be in the hold waiting for you both when you're ready."

Zersky went out of the shuttle's main cabin, leaving the two of them alone for the moment.

"Right, um, I wanted to apologize," Johnson said. "You know, for the awkward conversation we had right before the battle."

"You don't have anything to apologize for, Johnson."

"Please, call me Jane."

"Uh, Jane then. I was the one who misinterpreted what you were trying to say and made an ass out of myself."

"Yeah, about that. You actually didn't."

"Huh?"

"I did want to kiss you. I just got cold feet at the last second. I'm not exactly good at that sort of thing."

Bernhard chuckled. "Neither am I."

"But see, the thing is, we've got two weeks to practice and figure that kind of stuff out, don't we?" Johnson leaned over him. This time, there was absolutely no question about her intentions.

"Yes, we do," Bernhard said. And despite all the horrors this mission had provided, he suddenly found himself uncharacteristically optimistic about these next two weeks.

END

CHECK OUT OTHER GREAT SCIENCE FICTION BOOKS

FURNACE
by **Joseph Williams**

On a routine escort mission to a human colony, Lieutenant Michael Chalmers is pulled out of hyper-sleep a month early. The RSA Rockne Hummel is well off course and—as the ship's navigator—it's up to him to figure out why. It's supposed to be a simple fix, but when he attempts to identify their position in the known universe, nothing registers on his scans. The vessel has catapulted beyond the reach of starlight by at least a hundred trillion light-years. Then a planetary-mass object materializes behind them. It's burning brightly even without a star to heat it. Hundreds of damaged ships are locked in its orbit. The crew discovers there are no life-signs aboard any of them. As system failures sweep through the Hummel, neither Chalmers nor the pilot can prevent the vessel from crashing into the surface near a mysterious ancient city. And that's where the real nightmare begins.

LUNA
by **Rick Chesler**

On the threshold of opening the moon to tourist excursions, a private space firm owned by a visionary billionaire takes a team of non-astronauts to the lunar surface. To address concerns that the moon's barren rock may not hold long-term allure for an uber-wealthy clientele, the company's charismatic owner reveals to the group the ultimate discovery: life on the moon.

But what is initially a triumphant and world-changing moment soon gives way to unrelenting terror as the team experiences firsthand that despite their technological prowess, the moon still holds many secrets.

CHECK OUT OTHER GREAT SCIENCE FICTION BOOKS

IN PERPETUITY
by Jake Bible

For two thousand years, Earth and her many colonies across the galaxy have fought against the Estelian menace. Having faced overwhelming losses, the CSC has instituted the largest military draft ever, conscripting millions into the battle against the aliens. Major Bartram North has been tasked with the unenviable task of coordinating the military education of hundreds of thousands of recruits and turning them into troops ready to fight and die for the cause.

As Major North struggles to maintain a training pace that the CSC insists upon, he realizes something isn't right on the Perpetuity. But before he can investigate, the station dissolves into madness brought on by the physical booster known as pharma. Unfortunately for Major North, that is not the only nightmare he faces- an armada of Estelian warships is on the edge of the solar system and headed right for Earth!

BATTLEFIELD MARS
by David Robbins

Several centuries into the future, Earth has established three colonies on Mars. No indigenous life has been discovered, and humankind looks forward to making the Red Planet their own.

Then 'something' emerges out of a long-extinct volcano and doesn't like what the humans are doing.

Captain Archard Rahn, United Nations Interplanetary Corps, tries to stem the rising tide of slaughter. But the Martians are more than they seem, and it isn't long before Mars erupts in all-out war.

SEVEREDPRESS

 facebook.com/severedpress
 twitter.com/severedpress

CHECK OUT OTHER GREAT
SCIENCE FICTION BOOKS

SALVAGE MERC ONE
by Jake Bible

Joseph Laribeau was born to be a Marine in the Galactic Fleet. He was born to fight the alien enemies known as the Skrang Alliance and travel the galaxy doing his duty as a Marine Sergeant. But when the War ended and Joe found himself medically discharged, the best job ever was over and he never thought he'd find his way again.

Then a beautiful alien walked into his life and offered him a chance at something even greater than the Fleet, a chance to serve with the Salvage Merc Corp.

Now known as Salvage Merc One Eighty-Four, Joe Laribeau is given the ultimate assignment by the SMC bosses. To his surprise it is neither a military nor a corporate salvage. Rather, Joe has to risk his life for one of his own. He has to find and bring back the legend that started the Corp.

SERENGETI
by J.B. Rockwell

It was supposed to be an easy job: find the Dark Star Revolution Starships, destroy them, and go home. But a booby-trapped vessel decimates the Meridian Alliance fleet, leaving Serengeti—a Valkyrie class warship with a sentient AI brain—on her own; wrecked and abandoned in an empty expanse of space. On the edge of total failure, Serengeti thinks only of her crew. She herds the survivors into a lifeboat, intending to sling them into space. But the escape pod sticks in her belly, locking the cryogenically frozen crew inside.

Then a scavenger ship arrives to pick Serengeti's bones clean. Her engines dead, her guns long silenced, Serengeti and her last two robots must find a way to fight the scavengers off and save the crew trapped inside her.